RANSOMS ARE FOR AMATEURS

Ransoms Are For Amateurs

A Novella
by

JAMES W. WHITE

Adelaide Books
New York / Lisbon
2020

RANSOMS ARE FOR AMATEURS
A Novella
By James W. White

Copyright © by James W. White
Cover design © 2020 Adelaide Books

Published by Adelaide Books, New York / Lisbon
adelaidebooks.org

Editor-in-Chief
Stevan V. Nikolic

For any information, please address Adelaide Books
at info@adelaidebooks.org

or write to:

Adelaide Books
244 Fifth Ave. Suite D27
New York, NY, 10001

ISBN: 978-1-954351-26-4
Printed in the United States of America

For Babs

Contents

Chapter 1

Double-Wide

Cisco walked into his kitchen and went straight to the sink, sloshing across pools of rancid water and rotting food that lay scattered on the floor. The filth generated a powerful stink, but Cisco couldn't smell a thing.

He tapped on the cabinet doors under the sink. Three-year old Henry Peterson, a small boy, light- complexioned with pale blue eyes, whimpered from behind the doors where he lay, his neck chained to the drain pipe.

Satisfied that Henry was still alive, Cisco unlocked a cupboard door and pulled out a Polaroid camera.

Cisco's double-wide trailer home was the model of privacy and concealment. It was hidden within a warehouse, yet steps away from stores and services. The trailer was protected from the city's intrusions by heavy metal roll-up doors and industrial strength structural paneling. The exterior door featured a large sign with an orange and black bio-hazard symbol that read:

Surplus Contaminated Parts Depot

Authorized Personnel Only

The warehouse was located next to the city's Humane Society. Cisco loved to hear the dogs howl and he knew how to rile them up by throwing bones over the wall into the exercise area just outside their cages. Their howling was convenient from time to time.

A big man, Cisco measured over six feet if he stood straight, but he rarely did. A lifetime on the ragged edge of society had stooped him over, as if he carried an unseen burden. His neglected black hair hung long with streaks of gray showing through an oily shine. A smear of sweat across his forehead and neck came from a high body temperature condition that announced his presence long before he was seen.

Cisco made no effort to hide his cleft palate. No bandages or surgery hid the gash that substituted for a mouth. No lips hid his rotting teeth and gums. The remains of a tongue, ravaged during a jail-cell ambush by unfriendly inmates, turned his speech into a barely recognizable slur. To get back at his tormentors, Cisco had learned to speak clearly and he used his 'bilingual' skills to hide his identity. "My voice is my greatest disguise," he sometimes said.

"Yoo steel theer mii lettl frind?" Cisco opened the doors under the sink.

Henry shrieked as Cisco dropped to his knees and pointed the camera at the boy.

While doing ten years to life at Pelican Bay, Cisco had augmented his face with a patchwork of geometric and stylized jail tattoos. The ornamentation gave the impression of a disturbed mind, but behind that face, Cisco had a full complement of intelligence. An intelligence nurtured by a simmering anger that lashed out with howling fury whenever an unforgiving world reminded him that his life would forever be that of a loathsome outcast.

At the precise moment of Henry's terror, Cisco flashed two quick photos and closed the sink doors when he was done. "Thaats enuf, my lettl frind."

"Little pecker-head won't last long," Cisco murmured. The little boy was an unwanted surprise. Children were not his favorite victims. They were hard to manage and didn't live long. He preferred young adults with curb appeal, but this time, things didn't go as planned.

He scanned Friday morning's newspaper looking for an address.

It was always the same routine. The cops would play hardball while the media screamed outrage. They would search all the usual places and line up the local yo-yos trying to solve the case on their own. When they printed a P.O. Box address in the paper, he knew the cops were ready to talk. Usually it was the parents that forced the cops' hand.

The story was on the front page, along with a big spread about Queen Elizabeth's visit to San Francisco. The address was there, along with a photo.

Pictured above, Detective Helen McCurda, left, from the Bayview Precinct, stands next to Henry's parents and Henry's sister, Patricia. McCurda made the following statement,' "We ask for the community's help in rescuing Henry and apprehending the person or persons responsible for this terrible crime. A confidential phone number has been set up for anyone with information regarding the whereabouts of little Henry. Also, you can write, care of the following Post Office Box number..."

Cisco studied the photo. McCurda, must be new. She looks perky. Perky and stupid.

An inset photo of Henry looked very different from the Polaroids Cisco had taken in his kitchen.

While the Polaroids dried and developed, Cisco put on rubber gloves, threaded a sheet of paper into his portable Remington typewriter and typed the first letter to Henry's parents.

> Letter #1
> *March 4, 1983*
>
> *Dear Mr. and Mrs. Peterson,*
> *I have your child and, as of today, he is alive. Enclosed, please find evidence which, I'm sure, will substantiate my claim beyond any doubt.*
> *I do not guarantee your child's health or his life. But if you do exactly what I tell you in my forthcoming letters, I will guarantee Henry's delivery, dead or alive, promptly following the successful completion of my instructions.*
>
> *Sincerely,*
> *Henry's Guardian*

Cisco used a refined, highbrow writing style to mislead his pursuers. His technique of sending a sequence of letters leading up to the payoff was a chancy strategy. He knew any perceived pattern would be investigated. But the letters were important to Cisco. They gave him a chance to speak his tormented mind; to force his wrath on an audience who waited anxiously to read every word he chose to write.

The rubber gloves clacked on the keyboard as Cisco addressed the envelope using all capital letters. His baiting of the authorities was admired by his small circle of acquaintances. Getting away without a trace gave Cisco a reputation for being the best in the business. As an added feature, he enclosed a feces-stained swatch from Henry's Superman Underoos underpants.

He placed the letter in the out-box near the front door for his associate, Clyde, to mail. Job done, Cisco stretched out in his lounge chair, picked up one of the many newspapers that were stacked next to the chair and settled in to wait for mister fuck-up to come home.

With his sandy blond hair, medium height and build, Jacob wasn't a standout. But he blended into a crowd well and his congenial personality meant he could interact with strangers without causing suspicion, two talents Cisco valued in his team of associates.

Jacob wanted to learn the kidnapping trade and he had approached Cisco's organization to learn the ropes. Henry had been Jacob's first assignment. Unfortunately, it didn't go down well.

Jacob stopped in front of Cisco when he walked in.

"You looking for a job, pal?" he said, "or just reading the funnies?"

Staring at the newspaper, Cisco created something like a smile by moving his cheeks apart. He reached for one of the many pads of paper and pens that lay everywhere, scribbled a note and handed it to Jacob.

You fucked up my plans.

Jacob read the note and shook his head. "What plans? All we need to do now is collect the money and get the fuck outta Dodge."

Cisco once again raised his cheeks in mock mirth, but this time there wasn't the slightest trace of humor in his expression. He scribbled another note, wadded it up and mouthed garbled words that were clear and precise in his brain. "Weeers hees shoo?"

Jacob clenched his fists. He ignored Cisco's question and went into the kitchen. "God, it stinks in here!" he yelled while grabbing a handful of American cheese slices from the refrigerator.

When he shut the refrigerator door, Henry whimpered from underneath the sink.

Jacob twisted his cheese-filled mouth in disgust and shook his head when he came back into the living room. "He's gonna die in there. I'm tellin' ya."

"Shaadduup!" Cisco glowered at Jacob, "Da beeby is your fault. Noot mine. Weeers hees shoo?"

Jacob swallowed. "Fuck the God-damned shoe. There ain't been no trace." He pointed at Cisco for emphasis, "nowhere."

Cisco rose from his lounge chair and towered over Jacob, his face red. Sweat dripped down his face. He grabbed the pad and pen and dropped back in his chair.

I told you to cop the girl. That was the plan. You bring back a fucking baby. Where's the baby's other shoe? I'll tell you where his shoe is - the cops got the other shoe.

Cisco pointed back at Jacob. "Day'r traaace iiit baack too yoo."

"How they gonna do that?" Jacob shrugged and stuffed more cheese in his mouth. "It's just a kid's shoe, God damn it."

Cisco scribbled another note.

It's not for me to know that. It's cop business. They'll look at it and take pictures of it and dust it and ask people about it. Then they'll put it in a box with all the paperwork and attach a label on the box that says 'evidence' and forget about it.

Jacob chewed and smiled. "There 'ya go. Forgotten in some evidence cage, never to be seen again."

"Yeeea," Cisco said and wrote some more.

For maybe a year, or two, maybe. Until you're on trial for capital murder of little Henry. Then they'll pull out that box and pin the evidence on you. Maybe a fingerprint, maybe a thread, a hair. Enough to give you the big needle.

A piece of cheese stuck in Jacob's throat.

The snatch hadn't been perfect. Jacob had done all the preliminary work by the book. Cased out a park near a junior high school and watched it until he caught sight of a pattern; a teen-aged girl with her kid brother, alone while shadows deepen and just before the streetlights switch on, waiting for their pick up.

Cisco told him to take the girl. Distract her by luring the kid into the street. Yell a warning and when she runs for him take her. Use chloroform and a long loose overcoat. Stage it so you grab her near your car.

Jacob walked the park disguised as an old man in an over-coat. He ran Cisco's plan over and over in his mind, but each time he tried to execute something went wrong. Too many cars or people on the street, the streetlights came on too soon, the kid wouldn't cooperate, the girl started to act suspicious.

Afraid to fail, Jacob hatched a new plan of his own. When he walked by he dropped a piece of candy down the inside of his coat until the kid noticed it. A sweet pop in the mouth with dirt on it, just the way a three-year-old likes it. Forbidden treasure. One gulp and it's gone.

The kid got to waiting for the man in the overcoat and his treat. For days, Jacob pretended to pay no attention, just dropping the candy in front of the boy.

One rainy afternoon when the sister ran under a tree for shelter, Jacob slid the kid under his overcoat, taped his mouth shut in one deft movement, held him tight against his waist and moved to his car.

It was perfect. Maybe it was the kid instead of the girl, but what's the difference? The parents would be just as frantic. Only the boy lost a shoe when Jacob pitched him in the back seat of his car. A stupid, slip-on kid's shoe.

He'd gone back to look for the shoe. It was dark and wet by then, but he knew where to look. It had to be buried in a pile of leaves over a sewer drain. With the boy taped up under a blanket in the back seat, he used his flashlight and fished around in the leaves. Bingo, there it was, caked in mud.

He felt five seconds of relief until he felt someone tapping on the back of his coat. Startled, he twisted around and lost his balance teetering on the edge of the curb. When he reached for his car's fender to keep from falling, the shoe and flashlight went flying.

He recognized the girl, the boy's sister.

"Sorry to startle you mister. Have you seen a little boy around here?"

"Shit," Jacob muttered. He peered into the dark space where he thought the flashlight and shoe had landed. Behind him, he heard people moving about, calling Henry's name. "No. I ain't seen nothin'," he said, eyes still down, looking.

Following Jacob's gaze, the sharp-eyed girl spied the shoe and snatched it out of the leaves. "Holy cow! It's Henry's! I know it!"

"Hey!" She turned and shouted at some people. "I found one of Henry's shoes!"

"Stay right there, Patricia. I'm coming!" someone shouted back.

Patricia stared at Jacob while the sound of footsteps grew louder. "You look familiar."

Jacob jumped in the car and drove off.

He wanted to go back, but he envisioned driving into a scene of emergency lights. A fucking cop tapping on his window, a flashlight probing his face. 'Step outside the car, please.'

No. Better to let it go. It had started to rain again. His prints would wash off. Her prints would cover his. It was just a stupid shoe. Then he remembered his flashlight.

Cisco's size was convincing enough for Jacob to stop an argument that was getting out of hand. He knew he didn't stand a chance one-on-one, so he changed the subject.

"So what's the big deal about the kid? One kid's the same as another, right?" Jacob sat on the couch across from Cisco. He forced a smile, just in case.

Cisco grabbed another pad. *The kid won't live long. Needs too much attention. The time is cut short. No time for revenge.*

Jacob read Cisco's note and stared at him in bewilderment. "What the hell you talking about?"

Cisco's penchant for revenge meant nothing to Jacob. He wanted to learn how to execute a successful snatch and drop. Revenge was not part of Jacob's training plan.

Cisco grunted and got up from his chair. "Yoo got neew job."

"Huh?" Jacob gave Cisco a quizzical look. "Another snatch already? Shouldn't we finish?"

Cisco picked up the pad and jabbed out more words, *Bring me the shoe tomorrow morning. No shoe? You're done kidnapping, mister fuck-up. You get a new job.*

Jacob stood up but didn't move. "The damn shoe is gone, Okay? Down a drain somewhere. It ain't comin' back." He avoided Cisco's stare. "You promised to teach me the ropes. That's what I wanna do." He knew better than to mention the flashlight.

Cisco's face grew dark and his eyes glowed back at Jacob. A simmering rage emanated from his face. "U goonna doo I teell yooo, leettle maan."

Eyes wide, Jacob took a step back and shrugged his shoulders. "I don't know what you're talking about. I don't want no new job."

Henry started to wail.

Cisco's face softened as he got up and headed toward the kitchen. "Loook whaat yoo doone. Yoo waake uup baaby."

When Cisco opened the doors under the sink, Henry cringed in a fetal position, eyes closed. The shine of metal links reflected around the boy's neck.

Cisco grabbed a plastic trash bin next to the refrigerator and filled it with water.

"Tiiime feer shooower."

Henry opened his eyes wide.

"Thees whaat haapens too leettle booys whoo noot pootty traaand." Cisco pitched the water into Henry's hiding place.

The cold water struck Henry hard across his chest and knocked him against the back wall of the cabinet. The boy screamed from the cold.

While grabbing a key ring that dangled from the stove vent, Cisco saw Jacob standing at the kitchen door.

Jacob stared, wrinkling his nose in revulsion. "Why do you treat him that way?"

"Breeeks hiis spiirt. Soouunds beetr ooon daa phoon," Cisco spat over the sound of Henry's screams. He raised his arm, hand clenched in a fist. "Teel Clyydee throo doogs booones. Geet outta heere."

"All right, hombre." Jacob slammed the kitchen door behind him.

Cisco pulled a can of Spam and a can of creamed corn from the pantry and opened them with a butcher knife. Taking a dirty plate from the sink, he poured the contents of both cans on the plate, set it on the wet floor and slid it out into the middle of the kitchen. "Diiineer," He cooed.

The sliding plate made a distinctive scraping noise and Henry went silent.

Cisco chuckled while he dropped to his knees and reached under the sink. With a quick, violent movement, he grabbed the chain wrapped around Henry's neck and released the lock. "Ruun fer suuper, leettle maan," Cisco cooed as he freed the boy.

Henry scrambled toward the dinner plate. He spilled its contents when he slid on the wet floor, but he didn't stop grabbing for the food and gobbling up what he could.

"I don't wanna go in that dark place. I don't wanna," he said in between mouthfuls.

The cool, wet vinyl floor felt good on Cisco's bare feet. Memories of Pelican Bay came back. Security Housing Unit with its quiet, cool cells. He spent his hours in between exercise time naked, spread-eagled on the smooth floor, soaking in the coolness and thinking about his escape. At mealtime, the guards would toss his food tray through the trap door, spilling the contents on the cell floor. Cisco didn't mind. He'd drag a spoon across the congealed slop of potatoes, creamed corn and Jello and savor the taste of his sweat mixed in with the food. But when he rotated back to the general population ward, the memories weren't so good. He was welcomed back by a committee of five men who held him down while one cut his tongue in half with a pair of shears from the kitchen.

The medic on call the night they wheeled Cisco into the infirmary used a rusty needle and dental floss to sew up Cisco's bloody stump of a tongue. "Waxed," he said while he pulled the gash shut. "Don't worry, it's hygienic." He peered down Cisco's mouth with a squinty left eye.

When Cisco escaped a week later, he returned the favor, sewing the fucker's squinty eyelid shut. "I uusee saaamee floooss," Cisco whispered to the trussed up medic as he lay on the examining table, twitching under leather straps and Duct tape. "Dooon't worry, pleeenty leeeft." Sadly, Cisco was in a hurry and the needle missed a time or two.

"Diiner tiiime ooover," Cisco whispered. He pushed Henry away from what was left of his dinner.

"I don't wanna. I don't wanna," Henry howled while he was chained back under the sink. His howls changed to moans and then to silence as he resumed his fetal position, eyes shut.

Cisco retrieved his Polaroid and took more pictures.

Chapter 2

Wicked Fast

Detective Helen McCurda got to the precinct office late on the Friday morning of March 4 and found a stack of artist sketches of the Peterson case suspect on her desk. She appreciated the cup of coffee that was waiting for her arrival. Her partner, Sergeant Ben Bishop, could be thoughtful that way. She had to roll her eyes, though.

"Check it out, boss." Ben pointed at a sketch sitting by itself, next to the stack. He had scribbled a Hitler-like mustache under the suspect's nose.

Helen was in no mood for games. Earlier that morning, after finding out about Henry's shoe, she had interviewed the kidnapped boy's sister, fourteen-year old Patricia Peterson, and now Helen had a new and conflicting statement.

She took a sip from her scalding cup of coffee, grimacing as she burned her mouth.

The discovery of Henry's lost shoe hadn't hit the media yet, but it would soon.

"Doesn't he look like Hitler?" Ben smirked. "Total badass."

Helen sighed. "Turns out our man looks younger than Hitler."

She took another sip of coffee, knowing Ben's delayed response time.

He wasn't the sharpest knife in the drawer. What Helen liked about him was that he knew it and he was okay with that. They both knew Helen would put him down in a fight and he was okay about that as well. She had ten pounds on him at least. Not that she was a gorilla, he was simply too slim. She often badgered him to finish his meal when they had lunch together.

She was attracted to his brown eyes, mustache and hair that was longer than her chopped brunette 'do. Ben's wife had died during childbirth and he was doing his best raising a five-year old girl named Sarah while holding down a job that was often 'round-the-clock.

Helen was steadfastly single and liked it that way. Still, on the occasions when Helen would think about Ben as being more than her work partner, it was hard for her to come up with reasons why not.

She resisted looking at her watch.

Ben gave Helen a quizzical look. "Younger?"

"First go-round," she said, "Patricia told you the kidnapper was an old dude in a long, dark overcoat." Helen looked at another artist sketch from the stack on her desk. "I thought we were on to something because there aren't many old kidnappers. But when I talked to her this morning she'd changed her story. Last night, the family and some friends went back to the park to look around. Not only did she find Henry's shoe, she saw a guy in the vicinity that looked the same as our perp, only younger."

Helen took another sip. "Something happened last night. Same long coat, but was it the same guy?"

"Maybe he found the fountain of youth," Ben said. "He takes too many dips he might have to kidnap himself."

Helen laughed. "Now I *really* want to find this guy." She got up from her desk and studied a bulletin board. It had 'Henry Peterson' written at the top along with maps, photos, clippings and lots of notes pinned around the edges. After taking a long look at a map of Oakdale Park, she turned, a serious look on her face. "See what forensics has on that shoe. I'm going back to the park. Patricia's not telling us something."

McCurda got assigned to the Bayview Precinct station house six months earlier, following her promotion to detective. She had worked her way up the ranks using a strategy that promised success; beating the force's ingrained sexual prejudice with focused determination, willpower and a wicked-fast left hook that either stunned or laid you out on the floor, depending on her frame of mind.

"Nobody talks down to Helen McCurda," her chief had said during the ceremony when she was promoted to Detective rank. "And if they do, they're slow to get back up."

There'd been a ripple of laughter after Chief Albright made that remark, and a few heads nodded with acknowledgment. McCurda wasn't a theoretician, but she knew the policeman's handbook inside out and she knew her way around an apprehension. She'd handled every type of investigation during her years as a beat cop, more often than not the first person at the crime scene. There'd been a few tears, a few curses, nobody faulted her for that, but this was her first high-profile, media-centric crime.

When Albright put McCurda on the Peterson case there were some raised eyebrows around the office. Everyone knew

McCurda had been selected over seasoned officers who were more qualified. Nobody said anything, though.

"Get that sonofabitch," Albright said in the privacy of his office.

Helen nodded.

"You got one lead, Patricia Peterson's ID." Albright went on. "That's more than we usually get to start on cases like these. Use it wisely."

Now she had two IDs. Were two men involved? Or did a young man pose as the shuffling, decrepit kidnapper?

Oakdale Park looked empty when Helen pulled into a parking space and surveyed the grounds. Empty except for a dog walker and a groundskeeper blowing leaves from one side of the park to the other.

I hate leaf-blowers. Helen ignored the noise as she paced the perimeter of the park. *Kinda late for a park gardener to be working.*

There was the swing-set, where Henry was last seen. There were the picnic tables and the tree under which Patricia waited for her mother, the sandbox, the horseshoe pits and the pathway where the jogger ran every afternoon, rain or shine.

Everything matched up with Patricia's story. One minute Henry was playing around the swings and the next time Patricia looked up from her book, Henry was gone.

Ben had gotten the dispatch and picked up Mrs. Patterson before she left work. When they got to the park he was able to interview Patricia and the jogger. Patricia told him after she lost sight of Henry, she had charged out of the playground, worried her brother had toddled into the street. When he wasn't there, she yelled to the jogger to call the police. Then she heard a car start and drive off fast. She caught a glimpse of bumper stickers plastered all over the back of the car.

The jogger told Ben he heard Patricia's panicked crying of Henry's name and he had run to a nearby phone booth and dialed the operator. The guy remembered seeing the man walking around the park every day. He corroborated Patricia's description of the man being hunched over wearing a brown overcoat and agreed he appeared to be old.

When Helen interviewed Patricia this morning, Patricia told her she had gone back to the park yesterday evening with her mother to join friends and neighbors to search the park again.

"There was this man standing on the sidewalk." she had said. "I thought he was one of our friends. That was when I found Henry's shoe, and when I showed it to the man he ran to the car and drove away really fast. The man kinda looked the same as the old man with the long coat, only he was younger."

The car looked the same as the one she saw the afternoon of the kidnapping. She didn't notice the license plate, but she recognized the bumper stickers. "There were lots of 'em," she said, "with pictures of Jesus. Just like I saw before. And there was a cross hanging from the rear view mirror."

As she walked the park, something shiny in the tall grass caught Helen's eye. A can? Part of a toy? She kneeled down to take a closer look. When she reached in her pocket for an evidence bag, the groundskeeper walked past, leaf blower howling, covering her and the ground around her with leaves and dust. "Hey! Watch where you're going!" she yelled over the noisy motor as he passed.

He was wearing headphones and ignored her.

"How would you like a parks department broom handle up your ass, mister? The hard way!" Helen yelled while she wiped grit out of her eyes. When she could see again, the object was gone. She fished around in the wet grass with no success. It was probably nothing. She finished brushing dirt and leaves off her clothes and continued walking.

We got holy bumper stickers, a brown overcoat and a time traveler. How does that add up to a kidnapping? Oh yeah, and a crucifix, don't forget the crucifix. A religious nut who's in to little boys and disguises? Devout Father-and-son kidnapping tag team?

The leaf blower went silent.

I wonder what *he* knows? She turned and looked behind her, but the groundskeeper was gone. *That's funny.* She scanned the park. No sign of him. Huh? Two things, the shiny item and the gardener, suddenly disappear? Her watch let off an alarm.

"Shit," she said out loud and hustled back to the squad car. Ten minutes until Friday's press briefing. Her first.

Helen stopped her sprint to the conference room where the press briefing was being held when she heard Sally, the police department's public affairs spokesperson. Sally was speaking through the public address system. "Ladies and gentlemen, the officer in charge of the Henry Peterson case, Detective Helen McCurda, is temporarily detained. In the meantime, Sergeant Ben Bishop will open the briefing and take your questions."

Ben? Helen paused behind the stage curtain and chuckled. *You gonna handle this, partner? This ought to be good.*

Sally passed Helen on her way out. She winked at Helen and whispered, "You're a cruel woman, putting poor Ben in front of those alligators."

Helen smiled back and gave Sally a thumbs up. She peeped through the curtains and listened.

Standing behind the podium and squinting into the camera lights, Ben's face flashed an expression that said unprepared, un-briefed and scared shitless.

"Thank you, Sally," Ben mumbled while he rummaged through a stack of papers.

Reporters moved closer to the stage and waved their hands.

Ben took a deep breath. "Before we get to your questions, let me go over what we know so far."

"Atta boy," Helen whispered. "Dazzle 'em with your footwork." She put a hand to her mouth and smothered a chuckle as tape recorders started whirring, cameras clicked away and microphones on extension poles waved in the airspace above the reporters' heads, jostling for position.

"On the afternoon of Thursday, March 3, on or about five o'clock..." Ben stuck to the standard presentation format, but the reporters weren't buying it.

A young guy stood up, interrupting Ben's spiel. "Is Henry's father a suspect?"

Ben stared back with a blank look on his face.

Smelling blood, another reporter joined in. "Are there any other witnesses besides the sister?"

"Why hasn't the FBI been brought into the case yet?" Questions started flying from all around the room. "The kidnapper's letters are similar to the ones in the Tommy Winters case, can you comment on that?"

"Please," Ben raised his voice to a commanding pitch. The room went quiet.

Helen silently clapped her hands. "C'mon Ben, give 'em both barrels."

"I want to emphasize that our investigation is still in its early stages," Ben said. "We are following numerous leads, and at the present time–"

Helen stepped out and tapped Ben's shoulder.

Ben turned and sighed when he saw Helen. "Ladies and gentlemen," he said, gesturing toward his partner, "Detective McCurda."

"I apologize for showing up late," Helen said, addressing the audience. "My partner, Sergeant Bishop, has been on the Henry Peterson case since it opened yesterday and his investigative work has resulted in some key findings, some of which led to my late arrival today."

Lights, cameras and microphones all zoomed in on Helen as she moved next to Ben at the podium. She grabbed his arm when he retreated toward the curtain.

"Let me explain."

Helen waited for the room to quiet down. "Sergeant Bishop's initial interview with Henry's sister, Patricia, on the night of the kidnapping, established that the kidnapper was a solitary male who appeared to be past middle age." Helen paused for a minute while reporters scribbled in their notepads.

"He was wearing a long brown coat and a brown, wide-brimmed hat. We have no proof of this, but circumstantial evidence indicates the kidnapper may have been driving a late-model sedan, dark in color, with numerous bumper stickers on the trunk and rear panel, many of them religious in nature."

Helen took a breath and hands shot up across the room. She ignored them.

"I heard one of Henry's shoes was found last night," an energetic reporter spoke up. He got a pained expression from Helen for an answer.

Helen shook her head. "Since Patricia's statement on the night of the third, a significant development in the case took place last night during an area search by Patricia's friends and neighbors at Oakdale Park."

A hushed silence descended on the audience. All hands went down.

"An item of Henry's personal effects, namely a shoe, was discovered near where the kidnapping took place. The shoe was identified by Patricia and the parents as being Henry's."

Hands went up again. People fidgeted and murmured to each other.

"We have also learned, after a second interview with Patricia, that she found the shoe in the presence of a man wearing a similar-looking brown coat and dark brown hat."

People gasped. Reporters exited the room.

Helen spoke over the noise. "Patricia believes the man she saw last night did not match her initial description of the kidnapper despite the similar apparel."

Helen stepped back and looked at Ben, still standing beside her. "Sergeant Bishop and I will be heading up a task force to pursue these new leads. Oakdale Park has been closed indefinitely and is considered an active crime scene until further notice."

Ben kept his face to the cameras and avoided eye contact with the reporters.

Helen leaned into the microphones mounted to the podium. "Thank you very much. That's all we have at this time."

The remaining reporters shouted at Helen.

"Do you now believe there are two people involved in the crime? Was anything else found besides the shoe? How come the guy got away?"

"I cannot answer questions at the present time because of the sensitivity of the on-going investigation," Helen replied. "Our public affairs department will release a statement tonight."

As Helen and Ben turned to leave, a staff person came up to the podium and addressed the nearly empty room. "The next briefing will be announced when we have sufficient information to pass along. Thank you for your attendance."

"Tough crowd," Ben said while he and Helen walked through the precinct office building's front door. All eyes in the office bay turned toward them.

"I bet Henry's in a tough spot as well," Helen replied. "We got to get some traction fast." She looked around the room and stared back at the inquisitive faces. *They're looking for leadership.*

Turning to Ben, Helen raised her voice. "Get out an APB on any post-1970 sedan that has religious bumper stickers, front, back, top, bottom. Anywhere."

She walked to the Henry Peterson bulletin board, pointed at the map of Oakdale Park and raised her voice for everyone to hear. "I need volunteers to do a search," she said. Some heads nodded and some hands were raised. "Don't know exactly when yet, but I'll book a one hour meeting in the staff room for Monday morning and we'll figure it out." She pinned a sheet of paper on the bulletin board and wrote 'Park Search' at the top. "Here's a sign-up sheet. Thanks in advance. Oh, and by the way," she added. "This activity is confidential."

She walked back to Ben's desk and hung up his phone as he was dialing. "Don't mention the crucifix on the APB," she whispered.

"Why's that?"

"We save that ID until last. There are a lot of bumper stickers out there, but Patricia specifically said the ornament dangling from the rear-view mirror was a cross. The crucifix separates the wheat from the chaff, you might say."

"Roger that," Ben replied and got back on the phone.

Chapter 3

Preacher Man

Instead of first thing in the morning, Jacob didn't return until Saturday night. Clyde escorted him in an arm-lock. He had a bruise over his left eye.

"Yoo laaate," Cisco said as he nodded to Clyde to leave. "Stiiiiil noo shoo?"

Jacob shook his head. "I already told ya, it's gone." He tried to keep himself upright.

"Yoo haad ur chence. Nooow I chaange yoo iiidennntity."

Jacob saw it coming, but he wasn't quick enough to protect himself. The blows came fast. Cisco pounded at the cowering man's head. Rapid-fire, repeated punches to the head were Cisco's trademark, knocking Jacob against the door.

Bleeding down his face, Jacob's lip and ear split open and when his nose was crushed, the sound of cartilage and bone giving way resonated through the house.

Cisco took a few breaths, picked up the unconscious body and handcuffed Jacob to the sofa arm rest. "You gonna preach, little man," Cisco murmured as he made his way to his writing desk.

From the kitchen, Henry whimpered in a fitful sleep.

Letter #2
March 5, 1983

Dear Mr. and Mrs. Peterson,

I'm enclosing more evidence of your son's captivity. The pictures were taken on Friday night and I regret to say little Henry is getting worse for wear. Due to his delicate condition, it's important that you are confident my claim is legitimate.

As to his return, please read and follow the instructions I give in this and my next letter carefully. We all understand that any mishaps will result in the child's permanent disappearance. To confirm that threat, ask your police friends concerning the whereabouts of young Tommy Winters, previously from Saginaw, Michigan, a past acquaintance of mine.

To secure the future of your Henry, I'll need one-hundred thousand dollars in cash. Have the money made up of ten, twenty, and fifty dollar denominations. No ones, no fives, no hundreds. Do exactly as I say. Make sure your police friends carefully mark each bill. Put the money in canvas sacks and let me know when you're ready by placing an ad in the Examiner under the Personals column. The ad will read, Dear Tony, our flowers are in bloom and ready to be picked.

When I see the ad, I'll send you the next letter. I promise more pictures.

Sincerely,
Henry's Guardian

Cisco made a sigh of satisfaction as he folded the letter and addressed the envelope.

The game was on.

"Yoo knooo Gott?" Cisco stared at Jacob as seriously as his misshapen face would allow. A harsh morning sun shone through the warehouse skylight into Cisco's smeared living room window.

"What?" Jacob croaked. He opened his one good eye.

Cisco wrote on a pad and held it in front of Jacob's bloody face, *Do you know God?*

Jacob shook his head and closed his eye.

Cold water fell on Jacob's head. The water felt good on his open wounds, but the internal bruises and broken parts complained as he climbed back from unconsciousness.

"Preechr maan. Isss neew daay," Cisco said.

Jacob stirred. The handcuff restrained him. With his one good eye, he watched Cisco warily. Cisco's weird question confused him. "What the hell you talking about," Jacob whispered. "Do I know what?" He winced.

Cisco moved his table from under the reading lamp and set it next to the sofa.

While Cisco moved the table, Jacob reached down with his free hand and took hold of a penknife from inside his sock.

Cisco unfolded a map and spread it on the table. "Ef yoo noo Gott, maaake miii plaan woork bettr." He drew an 'X' on Montgomery Street, between Pine and Bush Streets, and held the map for Jacob to see. "Stuudy Bibl. Toomooro, yoo preech heeer." Cisco stabbed at the X. "Preech, heeeer, evry daaay."

While Cisco pointed at the map, Jacob flipped open the knife blade as he slid it upward.

It hurt like hell, but Jacob pretended to get a better look by sitting up. At the same time, he slid the knife up to his waist. "If some fucking evangelist got your soul that's your business, pal, but leave me out of it. No way man."

Jacob's current roommate, Sidney Felix, was a born-again Christian. At least he talked like one. Without any warning, the guy would start harping about Jesus and God's mercy and sin. It drove Jacob nuts how he would get so pompous and condescending, talking down to Jacob and telling him how he was going to burn in hell. Sidney did let him borrow his car, though, and he paid his rent on time.

Cisco opened the table's drawer and rummaged inside.

Jacob slid the knife in his pocket.

Cisco grunted and thrust a type-written sheet of paper in Jacob's face. "Reed."

Everybody thinks they know everything. The cops think they know the robbers, the robbers think they know the marks. And the marks, they're so stupid they think they know what's going on. But none of them know me. I kept Tommy Winters for two months, locked in a closet in a house with no neighbors. I fed him packaged food and drugged bottled water to keep him quiet. When he started to die I told his parents they could have the body back for twenty-five Gs. I made them stand with the money in a sack in downtown Saginaw all night on January 18th, my Mother's birthday. Fucking cops were everywhere, crawling around the neighborhood in their cars, but they never caught me and I never took their fucking marked money. I sold the kid while he was still breathing to a crooked surgeon from Bangladesh for parts. If you don't do what everybody knows you do, nobody knows. Ransoms are for amateurs.

Jacob looked up from the paper and shrugged his shoulders. "So?"

Cisco scribbled another note, *Nobody knows God. So God will play a part in my revenge and you will help Him.*

Jacob stared at Cisco's blank, repulsive face. There was no empathy. It was like looking into the eyes of a shark. "Give me a break," he said. "Guy Smiley was right, you are looney tunes."

Cisco made a half-hearted attempt to smile.

"Theet's esy frrr hiiim too saay," Cisco stammered while putting the paper back in the drawer. "Heeee's in daa piiin. Nobdy kaars heee saay nooow."

Jacob made a tiny nod of acknowledgment. Guy was in the pen, or probably dead. The inmates probably thought he was a Short Eyes, and child molesters never last long in prison. That wasn't Cisco's thing, Jacob could see that now. He wanted older kids because they had more value than just ransom money, they could be sold for snuff movies, or organ donors or for whatever hideous nightmares a high-paying clientele could dream up. But if you had a reputation for stealing kids, no matter how old they are, the assumption was that you liked to diddle with them and inmates with families didn't like to think of guys like you on the outside. Cisco had escaped, but he paid a big price. The prospect of getting tortured and killed if you were caught made kidnapping a challenge. Kidnappers who survived were tough. Jacob wanted to be tough.

"I already told you I ain't no God-damned preacher. Not for you or anybody."

In one lightening-fast movement, Cisco jammed a hand over Jacob's pocket, grabbed the knife and pushed the blade against his balls.

Jacob let go of the knife. The sharp pain in his groin took over the pain in his head. Eyes bulging, he held his breath and waited.

Their faces inches apart, Jacob finally had to inhale and he gagged on Cisco's rancid breath. He listened to Cisco's molars as they ground against each other in the back of his mouth. The knife probed the fleshy part of Jacob's groin, but didn't penetrate.

Cisco's eyes suddenly gleamed. He shoved the blade in the top of Jacob's thigh.

Screaming, Jacob tried to grab the knife, but Cisco pulled his free arm out of his pocket and pinned Jacob's hand against the table.

The knife handle stood erect inside Jacob's pants. The blue denim around it turned red.

"Please," Jacob whispered. His leg started to spasm. "For the love of God. Please."

Cisco lifted his cheeks in another ragged smile. He pulled the knife out of Jacob's leg, removed it from his pocket and let go of his arm.

He scribbled another note while Jacob clutched at the wound and moaned. He stuck the paper to the bloody knife blade and waved it in front of Jacob's battered face. *So you know God after all. That's good.*

Cisco cleared a stack of Sunday papers off his table, opened a drawer and pulled out a manila envelope. He spread the contents across the table and ripped off a sheet of blank note paper - *People don't care if you say religious words and say God once in a while. They ignore you. That's your new job.*

Jacob clutched his leg and peered at a stack of religious publications, *Four Spiritual Laws, Are You Prepared To Meet God? Help From Above, The Way to Happiness.* The titles made his stomach turn, but he didn't have room for more pain. They reminded him of his roommate. Too weak to complain, Jacob nodded and lay back on the couch. The cushion was wet with blood. "My leg," he said. "It's bleeding."

Cisco went to the bathroom and came back with a mirror and a roll of Duct Tape. "Jeest aaaa scraaatch, cryyyy baaaby." He handed Jacob the Duct Tape, positioned the mirror in front of his face and pulled out his writing tablet. *Look in the mirror.*

Jacob gave a startled gasp. He sat up and took a closer look. One eye swollen shut, nose pushed sideways, cuts and lacerations, cauliflower ear. It was hard to find anything familiar.

Another sheet of paper dangled in front of him.

I've given you a disguise. Now the cops won't recognize you. My associates tell me the cops are looking for you. The shoe told them everything.

Jacob closed his eye and leaned back against the bloody cushion. "Give me the God damned papers," he said. He wrapped Duct Tape around his injured leg as tight as he could.

Cisco got up without a word, shoved the table next to the sofa and looked at the kitchen door. The muffled sound of Henry's cries could be heard.

"Reeed peepers."

...The Bible tells us that all are sinners with no exception. As it is written, there is none righteous, no, not one. It also tells us that because we are sinners we are condemned to die, Except that a man be born again, he cannot see the Kingdom of God...

Jacob read until he fell asleep.

During the night, Jacob had fallen off the couch, knocked over the table and fell back asleep with the map over his face. When he woke up, Cisco's profile loomed through the map. His outline included a cup of coffee at the end of an arm. Everything hurt, but Jacob lifted the map off his face and pulled himself up on the couch. He dragged his punctured leg, flinching as he bent his knee in order to sit.

Cisco righted the table, sat down and slid the steaming cup toward Jacob.

Using both hands, Jacob lifted the cup to his lips. He looked at Cisco. "You ever read this stuff?"

Cisco made his hideous grin and wrote a note. *I know them all by heart. I collect them.*

"Seriously?"

"Believe what you read and you will be saved," Cisco said without impediment. He stood and headed for the kitchen.

Jacob dropped his cup and spilled coffee across the table. "You can talk?"

"Disguises aren't worth shit, little man. A second voice is the best disguise of all." Cisco stopped at the kitchen door. "Tell Clyde to get the dogs barking." Henry was due for another soaking.

Cisco walked back into the living room with deliberate, heavy effort. The howling dogs covered any noise from the kitchen, but it hadn't been easy. Henry had thrashed and screeched when the water hit him. "Jesus," Cisco muttered. "You had to grab a fuckin' baby.

Jacob grimaced in pain. His leg was throbbing and his face felt like it had been stung by a million wasps. His bad eye teared down his face. Fresh blood bloomed through the Duct Tape that was wrapped around Jacob's trouser leg. "I could use some first aid here. It's hard to concentrate with this hole in my leg."

Cisco ignored Jacob, opened the front door and came back with a newspaper. He studied the front page for a moment, then held it up for Jacob to see.

The headline read, 'Peterson Kidnapper Still At Large' over a photo of Henry smiling at the camera.

"Daa cawps aain't talkiiin'," Cisco stammered. He chuckled while he sat down and resumed reading.

"You talked like a normal person when you went in the kitchen," Jacob said. "What happened?"

Cisco rolled the paper up, leaned over and slapped Jacob across his tormented face.

The shock and pain stunned Jacob. He collapsed back on the sofa and moaned.

"Shaaaatup." Cisco pulled out his tablet.

Today you go on the street. Go home and wash up first. Clyde is outside. He will escort you to your location.

Later, Clyde reported that things didn't go as planned. "The little shit is wearing sandals, a black shirt and a hoodie. Looks like a God-damned monk."

Cisco dismissed his associate, returned to his chair and stared at the paper. *The fucker is going to get back at me by trying to win an academy award. Some bumbling cop will get suspicious and post a stooge to watch him. I can handle that.* He got on the phone.

The Monday morning rush hour along downtown San Francisco's Montgomery Street was nearly over by the time Jacob got his table set up. It hurt to move, and one eye remained swollen shut, but he concentrated on carefully laying out several of Cisco's tracts on a white sheet. A donations tin sat next to the literature. A small riser, hidden behind the tablecloth, allowed him to get his head above the crowd that flowed past him like a river of lost souls. After many postponements, Jacob stood on the riser. His injured leg wouldn't hold his weight and he had to keep his balance by leaning against the building. He stared at the tract in his hand and read.

"Hey folks! Did you know that there are some spiritual laws that govern your relationship with God?"

A passer-by flipped him the bird. Two well-groomed business women in pant suits pointed at him and laughed.

He scowled back at them, but resisted the temptation to say something discourteous.

"One law says that God loves you and has a plan for your life. In the Bible, it says: For God so loved the world, that He gave His only begotten Son, that whoever believes in Him should not perish, but have eternal life."

Jacob read the words in a flat, toneless monologue; no expression, no gestures, no emotion.

"So why is it that you are not getting everything you want? It's because another law says man is sinful and separated from God–"

"Speak up. Speak up, I can't hear you." The voice was barely audible above the traffic noise, but it caught Jacob's attention. He looked up from the tract and noticed a hand waving from across the street. A figure stood in the moving crowd, creating an eddy on the sidewalk, disrupting the crowd's flow. He was wearing military fatigues. "Louder. I still can't hear you." The figure fought to keep his place against the rush of bodies.

Jacob lowered his voice, hoping to discourage the guy.

"Another law says man is sinful and separated from God." The words sounded familiar. He had lost his place. He scanned the tract and began again. "You and I don't know God's love and we don't know his plan for our lives."

When Jacob turned the page, a grizzled man sporting a gray pony tail and dressed in military fatigues came up to the table. The man was holding a brown paper bag. The neck of a green bottle stuck out the top. "Here's a donation, asshole." The man turned his bag over Jacob's empty donation jar until liquid overflowed onto the table. It smelled like stale wine.

Jacob stood speechless as the old man gave him a gap-tooth smirk.

"You ain't no priest, and you ain't foolin' nobody, so quit pretending and get a job."

People nearby burst out laughing.

The man left as suddenly as he appeared. Dazed by the intrusion, Jacob sat on a window ledge next to his table and stared at the crowd passing by. The sun felt good on his ravaged face. Someone dropped a coin in his tin and stepped back in surprise when the coin made a splash.

As his good eye got heavy, a car stopped at the curb. The passenger-side window rolled down and Clyde, wearing dark glasses, pointed at Jacob. "Get in. Your day is done."

Somebody raced out from the back seat and collected Jacob's table and stack of wrinkled, wine-soaked tracts. He tossed the tin in the gutter and threw everything else in the car's trunk.

Jacob looked out the back window as the car sped away. His riser, left on the sidewalk, got in the crowd's way and someone kicked it into the street.

The next time Cisco fed Henry, the howling dogs were not necessary. The boy had dragged himself to his place of refuge under the kitchen sink without a sound. Sores and bruises were everywhere on his skinny body. The wounds weren't healing. Cisco knew the signs.

Jacob was wearing his sandals when Clyde escorted him through the front door.

"Father Jacob here didn't do too well," Clyde said when he dropped Jacob on the sofa.

Jacob grunted and held his injured leg with both hands.

Cisco nodded at Clyde. "Saaame tiiiime tooomorro, neeew plaaace," he said.

After Clyde left, Cisco pulled out his notepad.

You're going to a new place tomorrow. This time no table, no money can, no costume. Just preach. Never mind what people say or do. You got that?

Jacob nodded.

"Staaand uup, reed thees." Cisco thrust a religious pamphlet into Jacob's hand.

Jacob stood, but before he could focus on the words, he put his free hand over his eyes and sat back down. "I get dizzy spells," he said.

"Queet faaaking!" A dark cloud crossed Cisco's brow.

Jacob moaned as he got back up and started to read.

"In Revelation 9:13-20 the Bible predicts that one-third of the people on earth will be killed within a period of a few months. But God offers this hope to you today. Begin by admitting that you are a sinner, separated from God and are in need of his forgiveness..."

Cisco gestured for Jacob to sit back down. "OK, OK enouf. Dooo iiit thaaat waaay."

"I don't feel so good, Cisco. I get dizzy a lot."

"Shaddup. Yoo fuuckuup yoo nevr seee mee agaan." Cisco took out his notepad again.

Maybe you think that's a good thing. The cops will be nice to you, maybe fix your leg – until you're convicted and they put you away. Then they will forget you ever existed no matter how loud you shriek.

As Jacob got out of the car and staggered to the corner of Sacramento and Grant Avenue, a voice followed him from inside the car. "You better do what Cisco told you, boy."

Jacob ignored the insult. He made his way through the rushing, jostling crowd, his eyes straight ahead, At the intersection, he stopped and watched the people hurry past him. His throbbing leg consumed his consciousness. Bits of conversation and the traffic sounds flowed around him, but he took no notice. He pulled a religious tract out of his pocket and began to read out loud. He raised his voice, attempting to reach the people across the street.

"In the beginning, God created the heaven and the earth. He made man out of the dust of the earth and man had fellowship with God." Nobody hassled him. He drew a deep breath and continued. "Man was given a choice of good or evil; to obey God's commandments or disobey. And man chose evil. Disobeying God's direct instructions, man's fellowship with God was broken because God cannot fellowship with sinners, and man was lost."

Jacob was afraid about being watched by Cisco's associates, afraid a passerby might hassle him. Eyes down, he lost himself reading the words. Between booklets, Jacob looked up and saw uncaring faces pass in front of him. He let out a small sigh of relief and after clearing his throat, he kept reading.

"God will not allow sin in his presence, being a righteous God. Christ invaded our planet in the form of a man, born of a virgin. Because he loves you, he shed his blood for you and died on the cross to wash away your sins. Then he arose from the dead to become your defender. But only if you accept him as your lord and savior, will you go to heaven." The words flowed for the rest of the morning.

Cisco hummed tunelessly as he banged on the typewriter keys, writing out a new plan.

Jacob's stupid exhibition the day before nearly gave away Cisco's plan. Now he had to find a new preaching location, which meant new arrangements for surveillance, contact telephone numbers, money drop-off instructions and get-away route. The unexpected, last minute planning infuriated him and he slammed his fist against the desk top, spilling his coffee. *The fucker is no good to me any more. Damaged goods.* 'Kill the fucker after you leave the city,' he wrote in his instructions. 'At your discretion.'

Also, there were rumors about police activity at Oakdale Park. Another annoyance he had to deal with. He wrote a second note to Clyde who stood outside the front door. 'Find out when I can get to that detective bitch alone. And find out about that cop Bishop.'

Once Clyde left, Cisco wrote the next letter in anticipation of the ad he expected in the afternoon paper's Personals column. He wasn't disappointed.

Letter #3
March 8, 1983

Dear Mr. and Mrs. Peterson,

Pack the bills loose. No wrapped bundles, every single bill loose. Be in the ground floor of the office building at 260 Kearny near Bush Street at 8:00 am tomorrow, March 9. A phone at the reception desk will ring at exactly 8:30. Pick up the phone after three rings. Not four, not two. Three rings. DO NOT SAY A SINGLE WORD. You'll be told what to do with the money. Listen closely and don't ask questions. If the instructions are not carried out exactly right, my guarantee changes to a partial delivery. For his sake, don't fuck up.

Sincerely,
Henry's Guardian

Chapter 4

Pennies From Heaven

The shiny thing Helen glimpsed at the park kept going through her mind as she and Ben worked the phones all weekend. There had been the usual surge of tips and leads.

A mature-sounding woman had seen a man in a brown overcoat come out of a Penny's Department Store. He was having trouble carrying a very large canvas bag which was big enough to hold a three-year old. A man who identified himself as a city worker was worried about his neighbors across the street. "Some little kid over there has been crying constantly ever since the kidnapping story came out." A postal worker had seen a car with lots of bumper stickers.

"Thank you, sir," Ben said. He cradled the phone under his chin while he opened a package of Camel cigarettes. "Did you see the license plate? Started with the letter 'D?' Anything else?"

After Helen's search meeting on Monday, Ben had taken the rest of the day off to give his babysitter a break. The first day Helen could get approved for the search was Wednesday, years from now in crime-time. Something had to happen before then.

During a lull on Tuesday morning, Ben took a long drag as he hung up the phone and stared at the ceiling for a minute.

Helen put her phone down and took a sip of her tepid coffee.

"Hope I didn't get you into any trouble at the press conference," Ben said. "What held you up, anyway?"

Helen drew a geometric shape on a piece of typewriter paper.

"I found something while I was at the park," Helen said. "It was shiny, metallic maybe. I didn't recognize it, but when I bent down to get a closer look it disappeared."

"Disappeared? Like vanished into thin air?"

"No. In a cloud of dust and leaves."

Ben put out his cigarette. "You're always messing with me, Detective. Like a dust devil?"

Helen smiled. "Like a leaf-blower. Some jerk nearly bowled me over when I reached for the thing. When I finally got the grit out of my eyes it was gone. Funny thing is, when I looked for the jerk he was gone too. Here's what I saw."

She showed Ben her drawing of a cylinder-looking object. "It wasn't that big," she said. "About six-inches long."

"Flashlight maybe?"

"Maybe. It was covered with dirt so I'm not sure. Something's going on. I'm going to stake out the park tonight and watch."

"Could you use some company? How about I pay a visit around midnight?"

Helen's phone started ringing, but she ignored it and gave Ben a sweet smile instead. "I'd appreciate that. You did good at the briefing, by the way. Thanks for standing in."

Ben smiled back and stared at Helen's drawing, avoiding her eyes. A little color climbed up his neck. "All in the line of duty, Detective."

In the moonlight, Oakdale Park looked festive, festooned with yellow crime scene tape fluttering in the breeze.

Helen sunk into her cruiser's driver seat and kept her police radio volume low. She nursed a cup of coffee and looked at the park's blockhouse-like restroom. The image of being caught with her pants down in that ugly place by some teen-aged graffiti artist disturbed her. Better to use the disgusting 'policeman's friend', she decided. Even though her cruiser would smell like a sewer for weeks. She wasn't much of a smoker, but in case she needed something to cover the smell, she put a package of cigarettes Ben had given her on the dashboard.

News about the next day's search was officially suppressed, but Helen knew word would get out through unofficial channels. She was banking on it. The vermin would come looking, afraid the cops were on to something they hadn't foreseen. The Parks and Recreation Department didn't have any record of a groundskeeper that matched the description Helen gave them. In fact, Oakdale Park wasn't scheduled to be serviced for another two weeks. *Did he deliberately block me from picking up that thing, whatever it was?*

The radio crackled. It was Ben. He gave the signal to switch to his private channel.

"We got a positive ID on a dark colored sedan with religious bumper stickers all over the back end," he said. "Will let you know if it's wheat or chaff at rendezvous time."

"Roger that," Helen replied. She took another sip of coffee and switched off the mic. "Come to mama," she murmured. As shadows crept across the park's open spaces, Helen stayed alert by playing mental games. She was good at it, but tonight Ben infiltrated her thoughts. Ben and his little girl, Sarah.

I like the guy. Helen shook her head thinking about her cute, bumbling partner and his sweet kid. Did she imagine Ben had given little hints the feeling might be mutual? Could they become a happy little family together? *Tsk!* Helen scolded herself for imagining something out of nothing more than warm smiles and a handful of confidences.

A movement caught Helen's eye. A silhouette in the moonlight crossing between shadows. *I ought to call in*, she opened the door and slipped out of the cruiser.

The silhouette disappeared behind the blockhouse bathroom. She waited next to the vehicle, but it didn't reappear on the other side.

A trap? Helen released the holster's safety strap around her firearm. She watched the dark ground in front of her and listened as she crept toward the end of the bathroom building. At the corner, Helen waited a second, then quickly turned, her hand gripping the still-holstered firearm.

The blow caught her straight in the face, between the eyes, knocking her backward. She struggled to grab the bathroom wall when a second blow, this time to the temple, knocked her against the wall and dropped her.

When she came to, a shapeless blob filled her vision. Her wrists were handcuffed behind her back and she felt a heavy presence lying on top of her. One hand forced itself under her shirt and squeezed her breast while the other hand covered her mouth.

"Get off this case or I sell your boyfriend's little girl for parts," a voice whispered through a ski mask close to her ear.

Eyes wide, Helen mumbled. The pressure on her mouth eased a bit and the ski mask turned to hear her reply. She could feel an ear through the mask and she mumbled again, louder this time.

The hand over her mouth lifted, and that was the opportunity she hoped for. She lunged and bit down on the ear. She could feel the crunch of cartilage in her mouth. Blood dripped down the ski mask and on to Helen's neck. The hand on her breast moved out from under her shirt and she gasped when she heard a click and felt a blade press against her throat.

"Been nice meeting ya," the mask said.

"Detective McCurda!" Ben's flashlight swept the walls of the bathroom. "Helen! You in there?"

The mask grumbled. "Remember what I told you," it said. In an instant the creature was off her and gone.

"Ben!" Helen cried out. Despite her efforts to remain calm, her voice sounded shrill as it carried across the park.

"Oh my God, Helen." Ben pointed the flashlight at his partner for a second, then scanned the vicinity while he dropped to his knees. "You're bleeding." He took his handkerchief and applied pressure to Helen's throat.

"It's not me," Helen shook her head. A tear trickled down one cheek and spoiled her attempt at a smile. "You should see the other guy. He was huge. Handled me like a rag doll."

Ben removed the handcuffs and checked her for injuries. "Your head is a purple mess." He shined his light into her eyes. "You have a concussion." He got on his feet. "Stay put. I've got to call in help."

"Wait," Helen said.

Ben dropped back down on his knees. Emotions swept around both of them. Ben put his arms around her. "I'm sorry," he said.

Helen hugged back. "No," she whispered. "Just hold me." She held Ben tight and sobbed on his shoulder. "Hold me."

Wednesday morning, when Jacob hobbled out to the waiting car for his ride into town, Cisco was sitting in the back seat. He was wearing a ski mask. Dried blood stood out on one side of the mask.

As the car pulled off, Cisco dropped a watch and a large canvas bag in Jacob's lap.

"Stuuuuf iiin yuuur paants," he said and pointed at Clyde, the driver. "Telllll heem the plannn," he ordered.

"At nine o'clock, stop your preaching and grab as much money as you can," Clyde said. "When the sack is full, go around the corner on Bush Street. Your ride will be waiting."

"Money? Where's the money coming from?" The payoff plan had become a forgotten issue for Jacob.

"Noooo buulsheet quueestoons!" Cisco screamed.

At a stoplight, Clyde turned and looked at Jacob. "Just grab the money when you see it and run around the corner. You think you can do that?"

Jacob nodded. "OK. When money starts falling from the sky, count on me to snatch it up."

"Iiis yooour laaast daay," Cisco said. "Reeeembeer, niiiin oo'cloock."

Clyde cracked a smile as he eased up to the corner of Montgomery and Bush Streets.

Jacob sensed an air of nervous anticipation in the car as he pulled himself out.

"Did Mortimer drop the decoy duffel bag in the dumpster last night?" Cisco asked when they got back to the double-wide.

Clyde nodded.

"And he's at the payphone now?"

"Yeah, he's ready for my call."

"How about the dentist?"

Clyde nodded again. "I've arranged for Doctor Granger and his receptionist to be temporarily absent from their office this morning. I trust their patients will not be unduly inconvenienced."

Cisco grunted a chuckle, picked up one of two phones on the table and dialed a number. In the middle of the fourth ring, just before he hung up, someone answered. Cisco held the receiver away from his bandaged ear and scowled.

The voice on the other end blurted out, "I'm sorry I didn't answer on the...."

"Shut the fuck up," Cisco's screamed and began reading the instructions.

"Take the money to the third floor. Go in room 315, it's a dentist office, across the hall from the elevator door. There's a phone at the receptionist desk. The phone will ring in ten minutes, starting now. Pick up the phone and don't say shit. I will hang up after the third ring."

Click. Cisco looked at his watch, stood up and dropped his trousers to the floor.

"God, I love the excitement," Cisco grunted. He grabbed himself in front of a stunned Clyde and busied himself with his right hand.

"Whatever you say, boss." Clyde gave Cisco a weak smile and turned away.

When he finished, Cisco gave a long sigh, pulled his trousers back on and glanced at his script. "They'll play games," he said.

Clyde lifted the other phone's receiver and dialed the number of the payphone where Mortimer was standing by. "Window check in 10 seconds."

Cisco dialed his phone again. After one ring, someone lifted the receiver. Hushed voices could be heard in the background, but there was no greeting.

"Open the window that's in the examining room, the one with an X taped across it. Turn the phone toward the window so I can hear it open. Do it now."

He heard the sound of a window scraping through its jamb. Cisco looked over at Clyde, who listened to Mortimer and then shook his head. The wrong window had been opened.

Cisco chuckled into the phone while looking at Clyde. "Get the kid," he said.

He expected the cops would try to buy time once he gave away the window. Mortimer confirmed that plain-clothes cops were showing up at the Kearny and Bush Street intersection. Jacob was still preaching.

Clyde put his phone down, brought Henry in from the kitchen and dropped him on the floor at Cisco's feet. The boy lay still and didn't respond when Clyde poked him with his shoe. "He ain't dead, is he?"

Cisco leaned over and whispered in Henry's ear. "Diiineeer tiiiime."

Henry's eyes opened. He stared at Cisco, but didn't make a sound. Both eyes were swollen. He shook his head silently from side to side. "I don't wanna," he cried when Cisco grabbed an arm and twisted.

Dammit!" Cisco pulled Jacob's pen knife from a pocket. He handed it to Clyde, and spoke into the phone. "We're going to poke little Henry until he screams."

When Henry screeched in pain, a woman sobbed hysterically in the background.

Clyde got back on the line to the payphone. Again came the sound of a window opening and this time Mortimer gave the go-ahead. It was the right window. Clyde gave Cisco a thumbs-up.

On Kearny Street, ten armed plainclothes police took position amid the jostling crowd below the opened window at the height of morning rush hour. Other uniformed cops stood at the corners of the intersection, ready to divert traffic.

Cisco smiled and looked at his watch. It was nine-ten. Close enough. He got back on the phone. "Take two hands-full of bills and throw it all out the window. Now."

Clyde again gave the thumbs-up from Mortimer.

"Dump the rest of the money out the window," Cisco said. "Turn the sack upside down and dump all the bills into the wind. I want to see a green cloud fluttering out that window."

In the background, harsh voices could be heard. An argument of some sort. A woman's voice drowned them out. "Don't you dare risk my child's life with your damn police work," she said. "Give him what he wants."

Another confirmation came in from Mortimer. The money was flying.

Cisco continued.

"Your son is still alive. If all goes well, you'll find him after ten this morning in a green duffel bag. Look in a dumpster in Belden Place, the alley off Kearny Street between Bush and Pine. If we're not happy, you'll find large and small parts of Henry in trashcans all over the city." He slammed his phone down. "Let's roll. Put the kid in that duffel bag I gave you."

"Should I kill 'im?" Clyde asked. "He's just about dead already."

Henry's limp form filled the bag and didn't move or make a sound. A circle of blood appeared at the bottom of the bag.

Cisco paused a minute, then shook his head. "Haven't decided yet."

Jacob wasn't used to wearing a watch, it felt funny hugging his wrist and it distracted him to know that he had to be conscious of time. The watch also took away the identity he had developed while on the street. He was hiding something. He preached like he was told, but the words were a lie.

"...That empty feeling - like you're looking for something and you don't know what - like you're in a continuous forest, not knowing where to go and every day it's the same thing, day after day after day. Are you seeking answers for your life? Someone else is seeking also. For the Son of man is come to seek and to save that which was lost."

The sky grew dark. At 9:15, one hundred thousand dollars in marked bills fluttered down from a window above him. The effect of that much paper in the air was like a passing cloud. Nobody paid it any attention, including Jacob.

When the first bills fluttered to the street, the spark of recognition was instantaneous. One moment hundreds of people were mindlessly walking to work. The next moment the scene turned into a violent mob, grabbing and screaming at each other. Traffic came to a stop as people abandoned their cars.

Jacob heard the commotion and looked up from his tract. "So this is his plan," he said out loud. "Pennies from heaven."

Moving as quickly as his injured leg would allow him, Jacob hobbled in and out of the mob, knocking people aside and lunging for fistfuls of money. He grabbed until his sack was full and limped around the corner, looking for a familiar car.

Chapter 5

Officer Down

The crowd around him was acting like they were at a Niners playoff game; people were shouting, pushing and scrambling to snatch as much money as they could.

An elbow struck Ben's back, pushing him off-balance. He ignored it; no point trying to enforce restraint.

As the money cloud dissipated, people concentrated on picking up loose bills that were scattered along the curb and in the corners of buildings. Ben found it hard not to watch as grown men and women, most of them dressed for work, got down on their hands and knees and squabbled over the last few dollars that lay free for the taking.

The only clue Ben had was hearing someone say 'so this is his plan' after the money poured from the open window.

An hour earlier, he and Helen had got the call that the Peterson kidnapping case was reaching a critical point. Helen was in the hospital being treated for a concussion and numerous lacerations to her head and torso. Ben was at her side, going over last night's incident at Oakdale Park.

"Go, Ben," Helen had told him. "Remember, he's big and he's probably hiding his face because of his ear. Or it might be bandaged. I know for sure I took a chunk out of it."

"Yeah." Ben nodded. "Big dude with one ear. In addition to old kidnapper in a brown coat who morphed into a young kidnapper. No problem."

Helen gave back a weak smile and closed her eyes. "The more IDs the better."

"By the way," Helen spoke up when Ben turned to leave. "You sure Sarah is being watched?"

"It's her usual babysitter, Claudette, why?"

"Nothing really." Helen picked up her plastic cup of water to avoid Ben's stare. She took a sip through the straw.

Ben stopped at the door and turned around. "Should I be worried?"

Helen took another sip. "No." She shook her head. "It's just getting weird enough for me to be paranoid, that's all. Now get outta here."

Ben smiled back. "I'll be checking in, boss. Get better, okay?"

Helen put down the flimsy cup with an emphatic clack, spilling some water. "Catch that bastard. Make my day."

When the door closed, Helen called the Precinct office. When she hung up she shook her head. *I'm turning into a meddlesome almost-girlfriend. But with that beast on the loose, Sarah's going to need a lot more help than Claudette can provide.*

The beat cops had staked out the area around Kearny and Bush Streets once the phone calls to Henry's parents had started, but they didn't have much for Ben to go on. The negotiations were quick and the tech guys were having a hard time tracing the calls. Reports were coming in about people leaving the building without authorization, even though police had attempted to keep its doors closed. That was before the money started falling, after that there was no holding the people back.

Remote cameras had been set up at the drop-off location on Belden Place as soon as the kidnapper's instructions indicated where it was. So far, it was a no-show.

"So this is his plan, so this is his plan," Ben repeated the phrase as he paced the Kearny and Bush intersection. *Sounds like whoever it was, didn't know the plan, but he knew something.*

Behind his back, a man left a phone booth and walked up Kearny toward Pine Street.

The intersection was returning back to normal. People stared at the sidewalk and street as they walked by, but the money cloud had been picked clean.

Lying on the sidewalk was a small booklet. It had been trampled on, but it was still intact. Ben pulled out his handkerchief and picked it up. 'Hope For Hard Times' was printed across the front page. Behind the title was a crude drawing of a giant angel standing next to the silhouette of a much smaller man. Stars and comets filled the background.

"Shit," Ben ran to his patrol car. "The bumper stickers." He put the booklet in an evidence bag and tucked it in his notebook. When he got to the precinct office bay he spotted Jerry Shapiro at his desk.

"Jerry, you got anything more on that car with religious bumper stickers?" Ben had talked briefly to Officer Shapiro who had called in the ID last night. When he had to leave to spell Helen, Ben had asked him to write up a report.

Jerry handed Ben a typed incident report. "Dark colored Chevy Nova parked in the 700 block of Shotwell Street," he said. "Stickers all over the back and some on the rear doors. All religious in nature. Car is registered to a Sidney Felix. Address is in the report. No outstanding warrants or citations. He's clean."

"There's a carbon copy in the folder," Jerry added, pointing to a fat manila folder, labeled 'Peterson Case', that sat on Ben's desk.

"Did you notice anything besides the stickers?"

"Other than the stickers?" Jerry thought for a minute. "Well, one thing. It's a minor violation. Lots of people do it, but it's a pet peeve of mine. There was this cross hanging from the rear view mirror. Big thing swinging back and forth. Just waiting to bust his head in an accident. Guess he thinks Jesus will save him from the collateral damage."

Ben glanced at the report and nodded. "Thanks, Jerry."

Helen turned off the TV and adjusted her hospital gown when Ben came through the open door. She looked like she'd had an encounter with the flat side of a shovel, but she had regained her perky self. She pointed at a paper cup of dark-colored liquid sitting on her bedside table and shook her head.

"This weak, pathetic excuse for coffee they got here is disgusting, Ben. I can forgive them for rubbery lasagna, but–."

Ben dropped the incident report on Helen's lap. "We found the car."

Helen snatched the papers, complaints forgotten, and scanned the first page. She looked back at Ben.

"Crucifix?"

"Yup. Jerry didn't include it in the report, but he told me he remembered seeing a cross dangling off the rear view mirror. A pet peeve of his."

"Where's the car now?"

"Still parked at the address of the registered owner. He's clean, doesn't have any record, so I'm waiting on a warrant to impound the car."

Helen frowned. "Waiting on a warrant? Have you talked to the guy?"

"We've been busy with the kidnapping payoff, Detective. This guy... name's Sidney, Sidney Felix, weird name... takes second fiddle to what's going on downtown right now."

Helen frowned again. "Did they find anything in the park yesterday?"

"Beer cans, toys, wrappers, condoms, the usual junk. We did find a metal flashlight that matches the drawing you made, though. I sent it to the lab for prints." Ben showed Helen a photo of the flashlight. "Didn't you say you saw a shiny thing in the grass?"

"Uh-huh." Helen took another sip of coffee, gagged and put it back down.

"We found this in the sand box. Maybe a different thing or somebody moved it."

"Maybe the prints will tell us something. Anyway, that's the first good news you've told me so far. What about Henry?"

"No word on his whereabouts." Ben turned away and looked out the window. "The kidnapper orchestrated an elaborate distraction and appears to have made a successful getaway. We haven't had any contact since."

"So, I take it there was an arrangement to hand Henry over and the bastard didn't deliver."

"Yup. We're monitoring the drop site, but there hasn't been any activity."

Helen looked at the cup of coffee and poured it in a waste bin. "Where's the site?"

Ben turned back from the window and picked up a magazine. "A dumpster in the alley behind Bush Street, Belden Place. You know, where Sam's Grill is."

"Has anyone looked inside?"

Ben kept looking at the magazine. "The drop wasn't supposed to happen until ten o'clock or later. The cameras got set up as soon as we knew the location, so there's no way anyone could have –"

"Ben." Helen raised her voice and added a tinge of annoyance. "Put that down."

"Did you know that nine out of ten heart attacks happen in bed?" Ben lifted his eyes from the magazine and smiled.

Helen flashed Ben a look that put the magazine back in its rack. "You mean to tell me you're monitoring this dumpster and nobody has even looked inside?"

Ben returned a blank look. "Maybe somebody did when they set up the cameras. I don't know for sure."

"Jesus Christ, Ben!" Helen threw the blanket off the bed and started pulling sensor leads off her head. When her feet hit the floor an alarm went off.

Ben backed away and looked at the door, avoiding the sight of Helen's skimpy hospital gown.

"Where's your car?" Helen got her feet in some hospital slippers and wrapped a robe over her shoulders. "Sonofabitch," she mumbled and pointed at a closet while she reached into the side table drawer. "Get my clothes."

"I'm parked by the front entrance, but I don't think they'll let you out." Ben grabbed Helen's uniform and draped it over his arm.

A burly-looking man in a hospital blue tunic approached the door.

Ben stopped. *Here comes trouble.*

Helen removed her badge and firearm from the drawer. She took one step then hesitated as the aide barged through the door like a run-away truck.

"Put the weapon down and step back, please." The aide walked past Ben like he wasn't there, eyes glued on Helen. They stood face-to-face, both of them equals in size and weight. Both of them glaring at each other. "Don't make me ask a second time, because I won't."

Helen set her weapon on the table and held up her badge. "I'm a police officer, currently working on an active investigation. Time is an issue. I need to –"

"I know who you are, Detective McCurda, and you need to be in bed. You are under medication and in no condition to be anywhere else. Do you understand?" The aid looked at her like she was a public menace.

People stood outside the door, filling the hallway. A security guard made his way through the crowd.

Helen looked over the aid's shoulder at Ben. "You better get going," she sighed. "One of us better, anyway."

Ben nodded. He dropped Helen's clothes in a chair and gave her a sheepish look. "I'll inspect the dumpster myself."

Helen slumped her shoulders and, head down, stepped back toward the bed.

The aide walked around her, as if nothing had happened, gathered the sensor cables and started fussing with the control panel. Lights came on and a low hum resonated from the panel. In the hallway, the crowd dispersed as quickly as it had formed.

"Don't forget about the car and the bumper stickers," Helen said. She sat on the bed, kicked off the hospital slippers and looked at the incident report. "Get back to me if you find the driver."

She stiffened when the aide tried to coax her to lie back against the pillow.

"Anything else?" Ben asked.

"Bring me a God-damned thermos of Folgers Classic Roast," she shouted as Ben left the room.

As Cisco's car made its way down Mission Street toward the center of town, it passed a city bus going in the opposite direction.

"Turn around," Cisco said to Clyde, who was once again behind the wheel. "And follow that bus."

Two blocks later, the bus approached a stop that was crowded with shoppers carrying bags and boxes from the stores around Union Square. Clyde pulled over.

Cisco grabbed the duffel bag and dropped it in Clyde's lap. "Get Henry on that bus. Give him a nice seat all to himself."

"Hey lady, you forgot your bag," Clyde shouted while he elbowed his way through the queue of boarding passengers and up the bus steps. He smiled at the bus driver and held the duffel bag high, pointing at it. "You left it on the sidewalk."

Nobody paid attention to the Good Samaritan.

After Clyde dropped the bag on the bench seat at the back of the bus, he stepped out the back exit. The bag shook when the bus accelerated back into traffic, but nobody noticed.

Back behind the wheel, Clyde made a U-turn and continued toward downtown.

"Step on it," Cisco murmured. "Fuckhead is waiting with our money."

"Hey Vinny," Ben got hold of the crime scene coordinator from his car radio as he drove out of the hospital parking lot. "Any news?"

Sargent Vincent Fiorillo's voice boomed out from a clamor of background noise and static. "Nuttin'. No activity at the dumpster. Parents are getting hysterical. Looks to be a dry hole. What's with Detective McCurda?"

"She'll be in the hospital for another day at least. Head's banged up pretty bad. They got her on meds. I just left there."

"Roger that," Fiorillo replied.

Ben could hear screaming in the background.

After a pause, Fiorillo got back on the mic. "Anything else?"

"Yeah. Do me a favor," Ben replied. "Open the dumpster and look inside."

"The dumpster? What the hell for? We've been monitoring it all –"

"Helen thinks we're missing something." Ben interrupted. "Just do it, Vinny."

When Ben arrived, the owner of Sam's Grill, Gary Seput, was standing in the doorway of his historic restaurant, shouting at the officers that he needed to be open by noon. "Herb Caen is supposed to come over, Herb Caen! Give me a break here," Seput yelled. He could care less about the money that had blown around the corner from Kearny.

Ben jumped from his car into this chaotic scene. Ignoring Seput, he recognized a uniformed policemen, Patrol Officer Bill Chandler, standing on one side of the dumpster. On the other side, Fiorillo stood at the top of a step ladder, his head inside the dumpster. Chandler was holding Fiorillo's walkie-talkie, which was turned up to maximum volume.

Ben tipped his hat at Chandler's familiar face.

Officer Chandler nodded back. "Ben's here, Vinny."

"Get over here," Fiorillo said, waving in Ben's direction.

Ben squatted under the crime scene tape and approached the dumpster. Fiorillo let out a grunt.

"Shit." Fiorillo stood up, turned to Officer Chandler and grimaced. "Call the bomb squad."

While Chandler called in the request, Fiorillo gave up the ladder and Ben clambered onto the top step. He grabbed Fiorillo's shoulder for balance. On his tip-toes, Fiorillo pointed at a green duffel bag sitting in a jumble of trash.

"Looks like a bomb," Fiorillo said.

Still holding on to Fiorillo's shoulder, Ben set his walkie-talkie on the rim of the dumpster as a precaution and stretched into the cavity as close to the bag as he could. He strained to listen for any sounds of life over the noise going on around him, but heard nothing. "Shit," he murmured and shook his head. "How'd he do that?"

Before Fiorillo could answer, Chandler started shouting.

"Hold it right there, Mister."

Ben jumped off the ladder. Chandler had his weapon trained on a man standing near the other end of Beldon Place. The man was wearing a long coat and holding a sack. He twisted his head from side to side as if looking for something.

Chandler walked toward the shadowy figure. "Raise your hands," Chandler shouted. "Now."

"We got a camera pointing in that direction," whispered Fiorillo. "Should be able to get an ID."

A car slowly passed by on Pine Street, behind the man, and honked its horn.

"Getaway car," Ben whispered back.

The figure turned and limped in the direction of the car.

Too far away to nab the hobbling man, Officer Chandler took up chase, "Stop or I'll shoot."

The man turned out of sight on Pine Street with Chandler behind him.

A minute later, Ben and Fiorillo heard gun shots. One, two, three, a pause, then two more in quick succession.

Screams and shouting followed the fusillade.

"I got to stop," Fiorillo said, his heavy-set frame shuddered from the exertion when they reached Pine Street. He bent over, hands on knees gasping for breath.

His back against the wall, Ben released his weapon's safety and peered around the corner.

"Oh my God," he said. "Officer down." He reached for his walkie-talkie and came up with nothing.

Officer Chandler lay on the sidewalk face down. Blood was pooling beneath him and dripping over the curb. Fiorillo's walkie-talkie lay beside him. Traffic was at a standstill. People were huddled behind cars and in doorways. Cries and shouts were coming from all directions.

"Where's the guy with the sack?" Fiorillo said in between gasps. He reached for his walkie-talkie and came up with nothing.

"Don't see him," Ben replied. He stuck his head out farther. "Your walkie-talkie is on the sidewalk. Shit. We need backup fast." He ducked when the crack of a firearm from across the street followed an impact just above him. Shards of masonry fell in his head.

A bullhorn blasted from the same direction, above them. "Don't move," the voice commanded. "Or the kid goes out the window."

"Hostage situation," Ben said after he moved back behind the corner. "We gotta move."

Fiorillo nodded and stood up, hugging the wall. His face was flushed. "Yeah, but who? Where?"

Ben tapped him on the shoulder and pointed back toward the dumpster where his walkie-talkie rested on the rim. "Be right back," he said.

After replacing Helen's monitor leads and restarting the visual display, the hospital aide inserted an IV in Helen's arm and hooked it up to a bag filled with clear liquid.

"You're gonna get drowsy," he said while he adjusted the IV valve. "Just relax."

Helen made a sarcastic reply, but the aide's two-way radio squawked to life and drowned her out. "Code yellow, Code yellow. Active alert status. We've been contacted about a police action downtown. Possible injuries. All available personnel report to their work stations immediately for further instructions. This is not a drill."

"Shit," Helen said under her breath. She clenched her fists and fought to remain calm. Ben's face and that of his daughter's flashed in her head. Then the ski mask took their place. *He's out in the open. It's our best chance. I've got to stop him.*

The aide moved the IV stand against the wall and turned toward the door. "I'm not gonna be gone long. There's a security guard posted at the door," he said. "No funny business."

Helen nodded and closed her eyes. "I'm in no condition. I remember." As the door closed, she forced herself not to move while the sound of the aid's footsteps pounded down the hallway.

When she opened her eyes, the blue uniform of a hospital security guard stood outside her door, a walkie-talkie glued to his ear. He was a skinny, pimply-faced kid, probably earning some extra credits toward an AA degree in police studies.

Helen shook her head. *Security guard my ass.* She scanned the room. On a shelf above the bed was a roll of surgical adhesive tape. Not very strong, but lots of it. It would have to do. She put the tape under the sheet, grabbed a handful of towelettes, removed the sensor leads and the IV drip and turned off the visual display.

When the alarm went off, the boy looked in the room. Helen showed him her badge and beckoned him in with a big smile. "Hi. I'm Detective McCurda out of the Bayview Precinct. This damn alarm goes off every time I move." She pointed at his walkie-talkie. "What's this I hear about a police action?"

The kid's eyes went big when he put down the walkie-talkie. "It's going on downtown. People been shot. Sounds bad."

"Golly." Helen put her hand over her mouth. "Let me hear. Turn it up."

The hospital's public address speaker cackled to life. "Code blue. Ambulances en-route. Three gunshot victims. Critical injuries. ETA ten minutes."

When the kid looked up at the speaker to listen, Helen lay her wallet on the bed and sprang up behind him. She taped the kid's wrists behind his back and dropped him to the floor. Before he could scream, she stuffed towelettes in his mouth and taped it shut. It took her two precious minutes to find his car keys. "Sorry young fella," Helen grunted as she hoisted him into her bed. She taped his ankles and disconnected the call button just in case. After he was strapped in, she hooked him up to the IV drip and looked down into his terrified eyes. "This will make you drowsy. Just relax."

"I should have taped your eyes shut as well," she grumbled with her back to the kid while she stripped off her hospital gown and changed into her uniform. Just before she closed the closet door, she remembered her service belt, coiled up, almost invisible, on a dark shelf above the hangers.

She knew she wasn't thinking straight while she moved through a hurried, distracted throng on her way to the nearest exit door. *What am I forgetting? Got to move fast.* Outside, Helen took a deep breath of fresh air and set her walkie-talkie's frequency to Ben's private channel. "Bravo-six, Bravo-six," she repeated while walking across the parking lot, scanning the cars. "This is Helo-niner, over?" "Bravo-six, this is Helo-niner. What's your twenty, come back?"

There was no response.

Chapter 6

Helo-niner

Jacob squeezed himself in between the rear door and a man and woman who huddled in the back seat. The woman sobbed, her hands covering her face. The man, who sat nearest Jacob, clutched his upper arm, his face frozen in a strained grimace. A trickle of blood dripped from the seat to the floor.

Jacob crammed the sack of money behind the rear seat. He was out of breath from hobbling, his injured leg throbbed. All the windows were closed. The car lurched back into traffic while he let go of the money sack and struggled to get the door closed.

Cisco twisted from the front passenger seat and waved a pistol at the hostages. "One word out of you assholes and you're all dead. Understand?" The eyes that peered out of his ski mask were blood red.

Jacob nodded along with the others and stared out the windows. They were heading up Pine Street. A parade of cop cars and ambulances raced by in the opposite direction, lights flashing and sirens blaring. Gun shots popped off behind them.

Clyde chuckled when he stopped at a red light. "That Mortimer is somethin', ain't he? You got to admire his technique. Sittin' pretty up there."

Cisco grunted. "He won't last long. But long enough. You give him the bullhorn?"

"Yup. Plus two civilians and enough ammo to hold off an army."

Cisco nodded. "Trigger-happy sonofabitch. He shouldn't have shot up the place. We could have handled that cop quietly. Now, he's got the world on his ass. He's gonna need every round."

"Better him than us."

"Don't be so sure," Cisco said. He turned and stared at Jacob. "Your roommate still park his car in front of that house?"

Jacob nodded. "Yeah. But he might have driven it to work. Anyway, I don't have the keys."

Cisco nodded at Clyde. "We gotta ditch this car."

"Be there in five minutes," Clyde said.

Bingo. The car sat where it should be. The bumper stickers sparkled in the afternoon sun.

Clyde rolled slowly past the car while Cisco looked for stake-outs. At the end of the block, Clyde turned the car around and parked.

The temperature inside the car became unbearable in minutes. The man sitting next to Jacob let go of his arm and wiped his forehead, leaving a bloody streak.

"Where's the roommate?" Cisco said. The stink from his filthy, perspiring body consumed the car.

"I guess he's inside." Exasperated by the cramped, disgusting conditions in the back seat, Jacob breathed through his mouth. "What are we waiting for? It's hot in here, Cisco. Can't I at least open a window?"

"Uh-oh." Clyde gasped and shook his head.

"Oh for heaven's sake, Jacob, now look what you've done," Cisco replied. "You revealed my identity to these nice people." He pulled off his ski mask and showed his uncovered face to the hostages. "Whatever are we gonna do?" Beads of sweat covered his disfigured face, accenting the tattoos and cleft palate.

The woman screamed.

Jacob's seat-mate gave him a withering, side-long look.

"Oh shit," Jacob mumbled.

It took Helen precious minutes to find the kid's car in the hospital parking lot. She recognized the key to be a Datsun, and she focused her search on something cheap.

She found the thing in the front row, a beat-up B210 two-door. It was a tight fit. The driver's seat back was broken and was propped up with a stick. Helen had to remove her police duty belt to fit behind the wheel.

With the incident report balanced on her knees, she drove out of the parking lot. The suspect's address was not far from her location, in the Lower Mission District. Ben was her primary concern, but she was tempted to give the place a drive-by. Heading downtown, the light traffic convinced her it was worth the detour. *Shotwell Street, hope that refers to me and not to any bad guys. Car's gotta be impounded by now.* She did a double take and screeched to a halt when she saw the bumper stickers. "Well I'll be damned, right out there in front of God and everybody."

The street was empty. Nobody on the sidewalks, just a few cars parked here and there. Shutters drawn, a typical scraggily San Francisco urban neighborhood. A dog barked somewhere.

Why hasn't this thing been impounded? Helen squeezed herself out of the Datsun, glanced at her duty belt with her revolver and decided to leave it on the seat. *I won't stay long.*

The crucifix still dangled from the suspect car's rear-view.

As Helen inspected the car, a wave of frustration rolled over her. There she was, helpless in the hospital and what was her loony-tunes backup doing? Nothing! Didn't check the dumpster, kidnapper got away, Henry is still missing, people are apparently getting hurt, or killed maybe, he doesn't call her back and he hasn't even pursued this major piece of evidence. It's just sitting here. Shit, Henry might be in there.

"Hey, whaddya think you're doing!"

While Helen tried to force open the trunk, a screechy male voice coming from the house behind the car stopped her. She instinctively reached for her service revolver then uttered a mute gasp when her open hand found nothing.

"Police. Is this your car?" She shouted with as much authority as she could muster.

"What's it to you?" The voice answered back.

Helen scanned the windows and made out a bearded face peering at her from between some curtains. She remembered the suspect's description in Officer Shapiro's incident report included a beard.

Go get your belt. Helen patted her waist again.

"This car is under an active police investigation," Helen shouted. She walked back toward the Datsun. "I need you to step outside and answer a few questions."

"I don't see no police car. How do I know you're legit?" Sidney stood at the front door, opened now. He was wearing sweats, sandals and a tee shirt. A large Rottweiler growled and drooled at his side. Sidney held it using a choke collar and short leash.

Helen felt her pockets for her badge. She remembered grabbing her weapon from the side table in the hospital and holstering it on her way out, but her wallet with her badge got left behind. "Shit," she mumbled. Her head started to ache as the ibuprofen wore off.

Down the street, behind her, a car started.

Cisco watched Helen and stroked his chin. "What have we here?" he said.

"Looks like the cop forgot her cruiser," Clyde replied.

"That's not all she forgot." Cisco picked up his pistol from the center console. "Start the car." He removed the pistol's safely. "Not too fast," he added as Clyde drove down the street toward Helen.

Helen leaned in the driver-side door reaching for her service belt.

"Oh baby," Cisco mumbled as they approached the Datsun. "I got you where I want you." He turned to Clyde. "Pin her."

The woman in the back seat rolled down her window and shouted, "Look out!"

The shout made Helen jerk back out from inside the Datsun, belt in hand.

Cisco whirled around and shot the woman in the throat. The back seat filled with blood as she writhed and died on the laps of the two horrified men. Jacob cringed as the woman's dead eyes stared at him. The back window shattered and the money sack hung out the empty space, half in and half out of the car.

Startled, Sidney dropped the Rotty's leash.

"Sonofabitch," Cisco swore as Clyde approached the Datsun. He smiled as he and Helen made eye contact.

"You bastard!" Helen shouted as she scrambled out of the way of Cisco's car. Her walkie-talkie came to life with Ben's voice. "Helo-niner, Helo-niner," Ben said. "This is Bravo-six. Over?"

"Keep going," Cisco said as he tracked Helen with his pistol. "Nice and slow."

Past the Datsun, Cisco took aim at Helen through the back window. The two men in the back seat dove out of the way, shoving the dead woman to the floor.

The first shot went wide when Cisco's view was filled with the Rottweiler's head. The dog scrabbled furiously up the back of the car and lunged through the shattered glass. The second shot blew the dog's head off and ruptured the money sack. Bloody bills flew out the back of the car.

"Step on it," Cisco said.

Helen unholstered her weapon, took aim at Cisco's car and squeezed off two rounds, one of them went through the driver's door.

Holding his side, Clyde swerved the rapidly accelerating car steering with his other hand, tires squealing.

"What the hell's going on?" Jacob sat back up to see the dog slide off the car's trunk. He turned and stared into the muzzle of Cisco's gun.

Cisco squeezed off his third shot. The round grazed Jacob's temple, deflecting it off its intended target.

Jacob screamed and clutched his head.

"You're next, asshole." Before Cisco could line up another shot, the car's front right tire exploded, putting the car into an uncontrolled sideways skid, sending it up and over the curb.

Clutching his side, Clyde over-corrected the skid. The car spun across the street and up on a lawn, creating a shower of sparks and smoke.

As the car spun, Jacob slammed against the unsecured rear door. He grabbed the handle and the door opened. The next thing he experienced was a mouth-full of grass after he was hurtled out of the car.

When the car came to a stop, Cisco got out and pointed his gun at Helen. "You better answer that," he taunted.

Helen's walkie-talkie wouldn't stop squawking. "Helo-niner, helo-niner. Come in, over."

From behind the Datsun, Helen kept her weapon trained on Cisco. With her other hand, she switched on the mike. "This is Helo-niner. Over?"

"Helen, we're getting calls about gun shots in the vicinity of the suspect's car. I also got word you're not at the hospital. You copy?"

"Roger that." Helen replied, eyes glued on Cisco. "I need backup ASAP."

"Tell him his daughter's in good hands," Cisco shouted. He kept his gun trained on Helen as he side-stepped toward a house next to his disabled car.

"Put your hands up." Helen replied. The comment about Ben's daughter made the hair on the back of her neck stand up. She studied Cisco's face and saw a frayed strip of Duct Tape covering his left ear. *That monster who tried to kill me in the park.* Her head pounded and her vision swam. It was hard to concentrate. She shook her head to clear her sight.

"What's your twenty?" Ben asked.

Helen ignored Ben's call when a noise and movement caught her attention.

"Help. I'm hurt." From inside the car, a man waved. "Please help me."

Cisco sprang the moment he saw Helen look away. Between the car and the house, he took one wild shot in Helen's direction. At the porch, he put his shoulder to the front door. His weight and momentum busted the door's security chain like a twig.

A scream came from inside the house.

"Shit," Helen mumbled. She saw someone in the living room window, it looked to be a young boy. His arm was twisted behind his back. Cisco shattered the window and fired again, hitting the Datsun and missing her by inches. There was no option to shoot back.

"Helo-niner, helo-niner. What's your twenty. Over?"

Helen pulled the walkie-talkie from its holster and made sure it was set to Ben's private frequency. "I'm at the scene, Ben," she said. "The suspect is holed up in a house with a hostage, I'm pinned down outside and there are wounded in the vicinity. Need backup immediately. There's no one to cover the back entrance to the house."

"You're supposed to be in the hospital. What happened to that? Over."

Helen resisted the temptation to throw the walkie-talkie in the street. "If I don't hear sirens in the next three minutes I'm calling the National Guard. Over and out!" She dropped the walkie-talkie at her feet, never taking her eyes off the front window.

"I'm bleeding," came the voice from the car. A quick glance told her it wasn't the driver talking.

"Help is on the way," she replied. "Keep calm and apply pressure to your wound."

Helen let out a small sigh of relief when she heard sirens. She stuck her head over the Datsun's hood and looked at the house. It was silent and dark.

Shit. He's gone. Helen closed her eyes for a moment.

"Who were you talking to?" Fiorillo said when Ben turned off his walkie-talkie.

Ben's eyes were wider than usual. "Detective McCurda."

Behind Fiorillo, Pine Street was frozen in time. The man with the bullhorn was still making threats, traffic was gridlocked, moans and cries came from all corners, along with the relentless sirens.

Fiorillo grunted. "Yeah, so. She getting any better?"

"You might say that."

"Say what, exactly." Fiorillo raised an eyebrow and shook his head, waiting for an answer.

Ben glanced down at his feet to avoid Fiorillo's stare. "She's at the suspect's location, Vinny. Where the car is. She's pinned down. I've called in backup. Gotta go."

Mortimer's bullhorn blared from across the street. "I want a pepperoni pizza and a coupla' cans of Bud. Think you can do that?"

Another bullhorn answered back from the vicinity of the police squad cars. "Sure thing, Mortimer, comin' right up. You want cheese on that?"

Fiorillo cocked his head. "What suspect? Are these two things related?"

Ben peeked around the corner. A paramedic crouched behind a stalled car in the middle of the street wrapping a bandage around the leg of a screaming civilian. Helicopters circled above. Officer Chandler still lay face down on the red-stained sidewalk, twenty feet away.

Fiorillo pointed at the street. "We got the kidnapper pinned across the street, there. And he has the kid. What does McCurda have that makes it so important for you to leave?"

Ben backed away. "I don't know, Vinny. But knowing Detective McCurda, it's not small change."

Fiorillo nodded half-heartedly and waved Ben on. "Have somebody bring me a God-damned walkie-talkie," he said.

The first thing Ben saw when he reached Helen's location was the headless Rottweiler lying in the middle of the street in a pool of blood and money. Beside the dog, a young man was on his knees, crying.

At the far end of the street, a police cruiser, followed by an ambulance, were both in full code 3. They swerved into the intersection and barreled toward Ben.

The next thing he saw was Helen behind a brown Datsun, slumped to her knees, holding her head.

"Help me. Please." A voice came from another car sitting on a chewed-up lawn. Fresh skid marks on the street and the sidewalk showed how the car got there. There were bullet holes in the driver's side window and door panel.

"Helen. It's me. You all right?" Ben touched Helen's shoulder while he scanned the neighborhood.

Helen squinted in the sun and smiled. "You bring me that coffee?"

Ben stifled his habit of apologizing whenever he disappointed his partner. "You bet, sweetheart. What seems to be the matter?"

A policeman ran up, weapon drawn. "No hostiles. There's one deceased and three gunshot victims, one life-threatening. The medics are on it."

Ben nodded.

"Check this house," Helen pointed. "Be careful. There might be a man in there. He's armed and has a hostage."

Helen turned back to Ben. "So what was in the dumpster? And don't give me that sweetheart shit."

"There's a bag all right, but the kid's not in it. Some kind of diversion, maybe a bomb. I'm waiting for confirmation. Anyway, we got the kidnapper surrounded in an office on Clay Street. He claims he's got the kid and another hostage. We're waiting him out."

Ben paused and looked back at the street. "But the money. What's it doing here...?"

Helen shook her head. "Why would he do that?"

"Do what?"

"Why would the kidnapper let himself get surrounded?"

"He fucked up?"

"It doesn't add up, Ben. Kidnappers don't fuck up, at least not that bad. Sounds more like a kamikaze move to me."

"Kamikaze?"

"Yeah. A distraction. Somebody with a debt to pay sacrifices himself so numero uno can slip away."

"Some distraction," Ben said. "I couldn't count all the victims in the street, including Officer Chandler."

"Are you sure whoever that guy is has got Henry?"

"We don't have a positive visual, but the snipers confirm there's more than one hostage."

Helen struggled to get up, stumbled and clutched Ben's shoulder. "I wanna see..."

"All you're gonna see is that hospital bed, Detective Mc-Curda. You're way out of line as it is."

Helen shook her head and hid her pain by giving Ben a serious look. "I wanna see everyone from that car. Help me up."

"There's sign of a struggle," the policeman said when he reappeared from the house. "Whoever it was, didn't bother trying to hide his tracks. He knocked down the back gate and dragged someone. I've called for more backup. He can't get too far with an unconscious or resisting hostage."

"Have them cordon off the block," Ben said as he helped Helen to her feet.

"Better make it two blocks," Helen added. "The guy is a beast."

When Ben and Helen reached Cisco's car, the man with the hurt arm sat against the car bandaged from his shoulder to his wrist. Clyde lay on the lawn, face up. He was breathing in shallow gulps while a medic taped down the sterile dressings that covered the entry hole in his chest. Next to him, Jacob sat moaning, holding his bandaged head. His leg was bleeding again.

"I've covered the deceased. She's in the car," the medic reported.

Ben nodded and scanned the neighborhood. People were peering out from windows and partially-opened doors. The man Ben had seen weeping next to the dead dog, was walking toward them with a wad of bloody bills in his hand. "We're gonna need crowd control," Ben said to the policeman. "Help me string some tape."

Helen kneeled next to Jacob, but he turned away and wouldn't make eye contact.

"That dead woman in the car, she saved our lives," the man with the bandaged arm said. "She knew he was going to kill us. Brave woman."

He glared at Jacob. "You sealed our fate. Stupid sonofabitch."

"Who was he?" Helen shifted closer to the angry man.

"His name is Cisco," the man replied. "More like the devil if you ask me."

Helen turned and shouted to get Ben's attention. "Ben. The guy we're looking for uses Cisco as an alias."

"He's got a cleft pallet and his face is full of tattoos," the man added. "Looks more like a monster than a man."

"Yeah, Helen nodded in acknowledgement. "He did look odd. "You hear that Ben?" she shouted. "He shouldn't be hard to ID."

"Got it," Ben said and took out his walkie-talkie.

Chapter 7

The Mission

The bleeding had stopped and, although he was hungry and thirsty, Henry rested comfortably in the duffel bag. He lay in a fetal position, his thumb in his mouth, eyes closed.

He heard sounds and felt sensations while the bus stopped and started and stopped, a soothing rocking chair motion. The warm, moist space comforted him. People came and went, but nobody hurt him. The mean man was gone.

He tried to stretch in the dark space, but there wasn't enough room. He kicked and whimpered, but the muffled sound was lost under the noise of the bus.

Olivia waited for the bus at the Mission and Eighteenth Street stop, a three block walk from Saint Charles School. She was wearing her eighth-grade Catholic School outfit, plaid skirt and white blouse, white socks and loafers. It was the end of a warm school day and she had freed her neck from the tight bow around her Peter Pan collar and was fiddling with the top button when the bus pulled up.

"Bienvenido," the leering bus driver said, mispronouncing the word while Olivia dropped a quarter down the fare box.

Olivia returned a blank stare at the driver. She put her Sony Walkman headphones over her long, brown hair and headed toward the rear of the bus without comment. *Racist old white man. Screw your fake Spanish. Chinga tu madre, why don't you?*

Her friends would get on at the next stop and she looked forward to laughing with them about the despicable old bastard. She took an empty seat at the back of the bus and rolled up her waistband to make her skirt shorter. Her music rattled to a stop and as she turned over the cassette, she heard a muffled sound.

The duffel bag surprised her.

Olivia frowned and turned away. *Don't touch it. Some pervert probably put a frog in there.* She imagined a smelly toad full of warts.

At the next stop, a crowd of junior high tweens jostled around the bus' entry door, laughing and talking in fast, animated Spanglish.

Olivia stood up and beckoned them in. "It made a noise," she said as the girls streamed down the center aisle. She pointed at the bag.

Inez snapped her gum. "Olivia's found a duffel bag. Will wonders never cease. What's inside?" Inez sat next to the bag and wrinkled her nose. "A stinky genie?"

Embarrassed by Inez's affront, Olivia shot a menacing look toward Inez while the other girls giggled. "It's probably a frog or something."

As the bus pulled into traffic, the girls crowded around the bag and dared each other to touch it until the bag moved.

"Those of you in the back. For your own safety, please sit down," the bus driver boomed. His stubbled, pock-marked face filled the big mirror that viewed the bus' interior. He licked his lips and watched the girls intently.

A whimper came from inside the duffel.

"Shit," Inez whispered, eyes wide. "That don't sound like no fuckin' frog."

The girls dropped into their seats.

"It was here when I got on," Olivia said. "I think some-body left it on purpose."

"Well, duh," Inez replied. She raised her eyebrows and gave Olivia a snarky look.

Olivia bristled. "Well, smarty pants, what are you gonna do?"

The bag moved again.

The girls cringed.

At the next stop, an older lady pushing a personal grocery cart loaded with groceries marched down the center aisle. She gave the girls the eye as she sat down near where the girls were congregated then turned her gaze to a magazine.

Olivia slid the duffel bag along the seat until it was hidden from view. *It's a baby. I know it.*

"Open it," one of the girls said and reached over to pull on the zipper.

"Estupido." Olivia swatted her hand away.

Henry started to whimper.

Inez looked at Olivia wide-eyed. "I'm telling the driver guy," she said.

Inez stood up. "Mister bus driver man?" she shouted. "I think there's a —"

Olivia yanked on her skirt and whispered in a harsh tone. "What are you doing? Stop it! That fucker'll eat him for lunch."

The two girls glowered at each other.

The bus driver looked back at the girls through the mirror. "What is it, young lady?"

"Never-mind," Inez replied and sat back down. "Have it your way, chica. Don't say I didn't warn you."

"Quit fighting and just open it!" a girl sputtered. She reached over and slid the zipper open with a flick of her wrist.

Henry looked at the girl, squinted his blue eyes in the bright sunlight and smiled.

"Euwww," the girl exclaimed. "He smells like shit."

The old lady turned in her seat and frowned at the girls. "Please," she said. "No more of that." She cocked her head and sniffed. "What's that dreadful smell?"

Olivia pulled the 'Stop Request' cord. She picked up the duffel bag and cradled it in her arms while the bus rolled to a stop at Twenty-Second Street.

"Where you goin'?" Inez said. She reached to grab the duffel. "You're gonna get in real trouble."

"It's just my baby brother, ma'am," Olivia said, smiling at the old lady and tugging at the bag.

She jerked the bag out of Inez's hands. "He needs to get changed."

When Inez let go she felt something sticky and looked at her hands. *Blood!*

"Bravo-six, this is Victor-alpha. Over." Ben's walkie-talkie came to life just as more sirens filled the neighborhood. He recognized officer Vinny Fiorillo's call channel and pressed the 'send' button.

"Vinny. This is Ben. Over?"

While he waited for Vinny to respond, Ben gestured to a nearby policeman to approach Sidney from behind.

"Kidnapper shot dead." Fiorillo said. "Two hostages rescued. We do not have the kid. Repeat, the kid is not among the hostages."

"Roger that," Ben replied.

"What's your thirty-nine?" Fiorillo continued. "We've received numerous requests for support."

Ben turned away from Sidney's anguished face while he spoke into the walkie-talkie. "We're setting up a perimeter. Armed suspect is at large, presumably with hostage. We think this might be the perp."

A long pause followed. Then Fiorillo got back on the mike. "What about the kid?"

"No sign of him, Vinny. We're questioning the survivors."

"Survivors?" Another pause. "I'm en route. Out."

Ben holstered his walkie-talkie and looked at Helen for confirmation. She nodded back.

Sidney spoke up. "What's going on? Somebody shot my dog. And this money. Where'd it come from?"

"We'd like to ask you some questions," Ben replied. "What's your name?"

"Sidney," the man answered. He backed away a step. "What armed suspect?"

The policeman behind Sidney stood quietly.

Before Ben could answer, Sidney's face lit up with surprised recognition. "Jacob! What are you doing here?"

Jacob made an effort to get up, took a step and fell to his knees. His head bandage began to stain red and he gripped his leg.

"Cuff him," Ben yelled.

With two quick movements, Helen dropped Jacob on his stomach and cuffed his wrists behind his back.

"Please." Jacob twisted his head to one side and spat dirt out of his mouth. "I'm hurt. I didn't do nothin'."

Ben looked at Jacob and then back at Sidney. "You know that guy?"

"Know him? He's my roommate." Sidney gestured toward a house. "We live there. Is he in trouble?"

"Is that your car?" Ben pointed at the Chevy Nova with the bumper stickers.

"Yeah, that's my car." Sidney pointed at Helen. "I already told her that. What's so important about my car, anyways?"

"Don't say anything!" Jacob shouted.

As Ben and Helen approached Sidney, a look of panic crossed his face. "What the fuck?"

Sidney took another step back and when he turned to bolt, he ran into the policeman behind him.

"Hold it right there." The policeman took hold of Sidney's arm and twisted it into a half-nelson.

Two streets away, Cisco led a fifteen-year-old boy down an alley and into an open garage. The boy was barefoot and in his pajamas. He had a bruise on his left cheek and his hands were tied behind his back with an electrical cord.

Cisco flipped the garage door switch. Nothing. On a workbench lay the door drive mechanism in pieces.

"Mister?" The boy trembled. "I'm sick. Please don't hurt me."

A pile of oil-soaked rags lay in a corner next to a lawn mower and a gas can. Cisco picked one rag from off the top of the pile and held it in front of the boy's face. The boy flinched from the caustic smell and jerked his head back.

"You make one more sound, boy, and I stuff this rag in your mouth. Understand?"

"Uh-huh," the boy nodded, his eyes watered from the fumes.

Cisco pushed the boy to the floor and walked to the front of the garage. He looked up and down the alley. Police cars were parked at both ends, emergency lights flashing. He stepped back and dropped the clip from inside his pistol's hand grip. Two rounds left with one in the chamber. *Ain't no time like the present.*

When he looked again, two uniformed officers appeared at one end of the alley, walking a police dog on a leash. They were making their way slowly, moving from one side of the alley to the other. At the other end of the alley, more officers were standing and cradling long guns in their arms.

The boy smothered a sneezing fit. Once, twice, three times. "Sorry, mister," he said while he rubbed his nose with his sleeve. "I got a cold."

Cisco ignored the boy while he dragged pieces of furniture to the front of the garage. After he had a crude barricade assembled, he stuffed the oily rags in a cavity and doused the rest with gasoline. He waited until he could hear the police dog whining and the men coaxing him on. One flick of his lighter ignited the barricade and turned it into a wall of fire and black, acrid smoke.

The boy gasped as the fire sucked the air out of the garage.

Cisco fired one shot into the smoke and broke in the house, dragging the boy behind him.

The front door was wide open. Outside, a car's engine turned over twice then coughed and died.

Smoke from the fire blew over the house and cast a grey shadow across the lawn and street.

"Missus Hanson!" the boy cried, looking out the front door. Cisco slapped the boy hard, quieting him, and sprinted to the car just as the engine turned over a third time.

A woman sat in the driver's seat and struggled with the ignition. She took an extra second to depress the door lock, giving Cisco enough time to smash the window with his right fist and grab the woman's arm when the engine turned over and roared to life.

The woman sank her teeth into Cisco's arm with a vicious intensity that tore to the bone.

Cisco reached for his pistol. Tucked in his right pocket, it was an awkward reach with his left hand. After an unsuccessful attempt, he thrust his free hand through the busted window and grabbed the woman's throat.

The two were locked in a quiet, desperate struggle when a brown Datsun skidded to a stop next to the car.

Helen climbed out of the Datsun, weapon drawn. "Move away from the car," she ordered. Behind her, a police car pulled up. Ben and Officer Fiorillo climbed out.

With both of his arms in the car window, Cisco flashed Helen his hideous, misshapen smile. "That will require some cooperation from the driver." He winced and stifled a groan when the driver let go of his arm, taking a mouthful of flesh and blood with her.

The driver's head jerked back when Cisco punched her lights out after he let go of her throat. As he waved both hands above his head, blood poured down his right forearm. The Duct Tape covering his left ear hung loose.

"You OK in there?" Helen looked inside the car and opened the passenger door. The driver lay motionless across the front seats. Her long brunette hair covered her face.

"You have the right to remain silent..." Ben recited the Miranda Rights while Fiorillo pinned one of Cisco's hands behind his back. Fiorillo struggled to restrain the large man and free his handcuffs from his service belt.

Cisco's large, muscled arms barely reached around the back of his waist and he shuddered as the first cuff snapped shut around his right wrist. He sneered at Ben and resisted Fiorillo while the officer fought to keep his arms behind him.

"I've been informed that your daughter, Sarah, is in danger," Cisco said.

Fiorillo hadn't yet got the other cuff on when Ben paused in his recitation. Everyone froze.

"Sarah? My Sarah?"

In a flash, Cisco slipped out from Fiorillo's grasp.

"Watch him!" Ben yelled.

Helen looked up from investigating the unconscious woman as Cisco spun around and slammed the loose cuff against Fiorillo's face, stunning him. When Ben grappled to unholster his weapon, Cisco swung the loose handcuff chain over Ben's head and pressed the chain against his neck.

"Oh no you don't," Helen said. She moved around the car and faced Cisco. "Not this time."

"Have you ever heard a neck snap?" Cisco said. "Considering the significance of the event, it's a pathetic sound."

He jerked Ben up until he was on his tip-toes, his hands clawing at his neck.

Helen walked toward Cisco, forcing herself to keep a calm, composed look on her face. She stopped when she saw he was having trouble.

Cisco's shoulders were trembling from the strain. The bite wound was sapping his strength. He tried to hide his condition, but the pain was evident in his eyes.

Helen glanced at Fiorillo. He was regaining his composure despite a fresh gash that traced across his temple. "Shoot him," she said.

Ben shielded Cisco, but Fiorillo took careful aim and squeezed off a round.

Cisco's right elbow exploded in a red ball and Ben dropped to the ground. Cisco clutched what was left of his elbow and grunted.

Gasping for breath, Ben scrambled out of Cisco's way.

With a low moan, Cisco sunk to his knees. He tried to reach for his pistol, but once again he couldn't get to his right pocket with his left hand. He gave up trying and stared at Helen like a bloodied bull contemplating a last attempt on the matador. His right arm and what was left of his right elbow was bleeding down his side.

"You know why I didn't slit your throat that night at the park? You squirmed under my cock, that's why. You loved it."

Cisco laughed a hard, raucous laugh. "And when I get out, you'll be waiting for me. I'll be the best fuck you'll ever have."

He looked at Ben and snorted. "Little shit of a man ain't gonna satisfy the likes of you."

Helen stood her ground in front of the beast and kept a neutral look on her face while Fiorillo sighted his weapon on Cisco from a few steps away. Two more squad cars screeched to a stop in front of the scene. "Where's Henry?" was all she said.

"Soom booody u knoooo?" he rumbled back.

Cisco was barely able to walk as he was dragged away, nearly toppling the two cops who gripped him from both sides.

"Helen," Ben said as he struggled to his feet. He hesitated in embarrassment after calling Helen by her first name while on duty. Purple chain marks stood out around his neck. "Detective," he started again. "What about Sarah? Has he done something...?"

Helen looked closely at the chain marks, but avoided Ben's eyes. Her head was pounding again as the adrenalin wore off. "Sarah's at the Precinct office, Ben." She forced herself to smile. "I had Jerry pick her up this morning. Just in case."

Olivia watched all the girls stare at her out the back window as the bus pulled away. She stuck out her tongue behind the blue cloud of exhaust. "I'll take care of you later!" she shouted.

Under her arm, Henry stretched and smiled and thrust an arm toward her. She struggled to hold the duffel bag tight against her side.

"Out," Henry said. He stared at Olivia and blinked his eyes in contentment.

Olivia glanced up and down busy Mission Street. "Holy shit, what am I gonna do with you?" A squad car cruised by, its police radio blaring. The two officers scanned the sidewalks with scowls on their faces, searching for something.

"Don't look at 'em," Olivia murmured.

Head down, she walked quickly to the next block and turned left into a dense neighborhood crowded with apartments, bodegas, liquor stores and restaurants. Shadows were filling in the street along with the smells of dinner being prepared in Cuban, Mexican, South American and Caribbean kitchens. Laughter and conversation in a multitude of languages streamed out open doors and windows.

Olivia tried to relax as she slowed down her pace. She was safe and at home, but the baby boy was getting heavy and the enormity of what she'd done began to settle in. She shifted the load to her other arm as she walked. *Tia Rosa, she'll know what to do.*

A block later, Olivia stopped in front of a two-story apartment building. She took one more look up and down the street, climbed the front steps and rang the bell on one of the three front doors. "Come on, little man," she said. Through the door came the sound of children playing.

"You are insane!" Rosa screeched when Olivia lay the Henry on a changing table. On the wall over the table a sign read, 'Rosa's Day Care Center.'

Henry stared back at Rosa and Olivia and gurgled.

"Insane and stupid!" Rosa added. "You can't just drop some strange kid on my doorstep like a bottle of milk! Look at him. He's bleeding ferchristsake."

Olivia cringed and stared at the floor. "Tia. He was abandoned on the bus. Inez wanted to turn him over to the bus driver and, and..."

"And why not?" Rosa lifted Henry out of the bag and made a face. "Whew! You need a change bad."

"Because he's a disgusting, four-hundred pound faggot who'll eat him for lunch."

Experienced hands removed Henry's soiled overalls, wiped the shitty slime off his skinny, bruised body and cleaned the dried blood around the puncture wound on his leg. "He wouldn't make much of a meal. Looks like he hasn't been treated very well."

Olivia stepped back and waved her hand in front of her face to block the smell. Two young girls toddled over from the play area to investigate. "Poopy pants," they said.

"Don't you understand?" Rosa said while she fitted Henry with a fresh diaper. "I don't have a license. If anyone found out I was harboring an abandoned kid I'd lose my business and go to jail, especially a white kid. God help me."

"But Tia," Olivia took Henry's overalls from Rosa's out-stretched fingers and dropped them in a garbage pail, "I thought maybe you could find somebody who wants a baby."

"You thought sooo wrong," Rosa replied. She set Henry on the floor with two other babies, each with a cracker in their hands. "Now I'll have to go to Child Welfare Services, fill out forms and shit, answer embarrassing questions. What am I going to tell them? You're turning my life into a nightmare, honey."

Henry crawled close to one of the babies and reached for a cracker.

"Look at that. He's hungry. Probably hasn't eaten in days." She handed Olivia a small bowl of creamed spinach from the kitchen counter. "Do something useful."

"Si, Tia." Olivia tried to please her aunt by obediently sit-ting on the floor. She put Henry in her lap and began to spoon feed him. Henry eagerly slurped the food. "He's such a cutie. There must be somebody –"

Henry reached out and knocked the spinach bowl out of her hands. He squirmed out of Olivia's lap and stretched out on the floor licking the food. He spread pieces of spinach on his chest. Shaking his head and tight-fisted, he beat against

Olivia's hands when she tried to pick him up. "I don't wanna, I don't wanna," he screamed.

"Dios mio," Rosa whispered, watching Henry, her eyes open wide. "Where did he learn that, I wonder."

About the Author

James W. White is a California-based writer of historical and science fiction. He earned an MA in U.S. History. His profes-sional career has included military service, teaching, research librarian and technical writing. Jim's stories have appeared in *Datura Literary Journal, Chronoscope Magazine, The Wapshott Press* and *Scarlet Leaf Review.*